CURSED

AN URBAN FANTASY

BOUND BY SHADOWS
BOOK TWO

ANN GIMPEL

CONTENTS

CURSED

BOUND BY SHADOWS, BOOK TWO

Urban Fantasy

By

Ann Gimpel

Tumble off reality's edge into a cruel world where only the perfect are valued.

Copyright Page

BOOK DESCRIPTION, CURSED:

Magic runs strong in me, but power isn't enough.

I've traveled a long road since the Coven kicked me out. It's only been a matter of weeks, but it may as well be years. I've learned a lot, and nothing at all. One thing's for certain: my life up until now has been a sham.

My wolf, beloved familiar, knew far more than he disclosed. Hard to fault him since he was trying to keep me safe. Mother, the one witch who could have shed light on my origins, is dead.

Try as I might, I couldn't save her.

Along the way, a Fae took me under his wing, but it's confusing. Damien says he loves me. I have no idea what I feel beyond sorrow and anger. All I want is to torch the Coven guild house, avenge Mother's death, and locate Hecate, goddess of witches.

Secrets of my origins lie within her. Secrets forged

centuries ago. At one time, I was important to her, critical enough to bend rules.

She's abandoned me too, except she doesn't get to walk away.

I will find her and demand answers.

Answers to shape the rest of my existence.

BOOKS IN THE BOUND BY SHADOWS SERIES:

Scarred, Book One
Cursed, Book Two
Promised, Book Three

AUTHOR'S NOTE:

When I finished Grigori, last of the Circle of Assassin books, I surveyed my newsletter subscribers to determine what to write next. I may have gone overboard this last Black Friday, but I now have covers for three very different series. Covers are always an author's rate limiting step, so I stock up when I can.

The consensus amongst my newsletter group was they wanted the misfit witch series. A reaper series, Urban Sisters, came in second. A dystopian series, Shattered Worlds, was a distant third. Gosh, wonder if I'll ever get around to writing that one.

I love plotting out brand new series. Who will the characters be? Where will it take place? Will the world be open (e.g. humans know about magic) or closed? Will there be portals?

So many directions.

Book one is done. Onward to *Cursed*, book two of Bound by Shadows.

CHAPTER ONE, MORGAN

Zeke, white wolf and beloved familiar, pranced by my side. We'd taken advantage of a rare sunny afternoon in the Pacific Northwest to stretch our legs and soak in the beauty of the natural world.

Witches are its guardians, or I thought we were.

Regardless how many of my erstwhile witch sisters have slid off the rails, I still value every plant, every animal, every crystal, every rock.

With a sideways leap, Zeke pounced and surfaced with something small and wriggling clamped between his jaws. A few crunches, and it disappeared down his gullet.

"Whoa. Slow down," I teased. "What is that? Number ten?"

"*Twelve,*" he informed me solemnly. "*Who knows when the hunting will be this plentiful again.*"

It was true. Damien, a Fae who'd been in the right place at the right time to keep my world from turning into a total shitshow, was on the prowl for somewhere we could hole up for a while. Our current location, a rustic cabin in the southern Cascade Range, wouldn't do for more than a night or two. No heat beyond a stone hearth. No food. No bedding.

Not that we couldn't procure the latter two, but Damien was convinced we could do better.

Zeke finished swallowing. *"You were different,"* he said.

I slowed and glanced at him. He's a big guy, close to 150 pounds of solid muscle with almond-shaped eyes, one dark and one white just like me.

"Different when?"

"When you were killing all those witches."

His words sat like stones between us. I kept walking. "Didn't realize I'd gone that far," I told him. "Only meant to teach them a lesson for spying on us and scattering their dirty, nasty hex bags around. Besides, witches are supposed to be immortal. It never occurred to me I could kill them even if I'd wanted to."

"Your magic is different." He qualified his earlier statement.

This time I stopped dead. "Even now?"

Zeke flopped his head up and down. *"Go ahead. Test it."*

Wasting magic went against my principles. Unless I had a solid use for my skills, I kept them under wraps.

"We could teleport back to the cabin." His gaze zeroed in on mine.

The sun skirted the western horizon. It would be dark soon. I'd had such a pleasant time exploring a new area—one with no witches or mortals—I'd lost track of time.

I hadn't actually deployed my ability since the debacle

outside the boardinghouse. By the time Damien scooted us out of there, the street was saturated with police, ambulances, and the dreaded PDA wagon. I'd never given much thought to the Paranormal Detective Agency when I lived with my Coven—

Not mine any longer, I corrected myself.

Back to the PDA. It's staffed by mages, according to Damien. Meant they had power of their own and tracking skills. Before we'd left, Damien scoured my room and the rest of the lodging of any trace of my magic.

Even if he hadn't, the PDA would have to be formidable to find me all the way out here.

"Well?" Zeke nudged me with his snout.

It wasn't a bad suggestion. We were miles from the cottage. I hadn't planned well, but the past days had been so stressful, a break was welcome, even needed. Given a do-over, I'd probably repeat my actions.

I gathered the makings of a transport spell and visualized the small wooden structure Damien had taken us to the previous night. Zeke leaned against me to make it easy to include him.

All the pieces jumped to my command. Unusual, but not unheard of. I kindled my casting. Results were instantaneous. One moment, we stood in the forest. The next, we were in front of our destination.

Breath swooshed from me; I sank into a crouch.

"See?" Zeke's tail plumed. He padded to a nearby creek and drank deeply.

No. I did not "see." Magic has been a constant all my long life. Suddenly, I was stronger by a factor of maybe five.

Or even ten.

I'd barely thought my transport spell, and here we were.

Damien had been right about me taking care slinging magic about until I had a much better handle on my newfound talent.

After pushing to my feet, I trudged up the steps deep in thought. I'd build a fire and do my damnedest to sort through this new development. Annihilating the witches should have been a wakeup call, but I'd been too wrapped up in retribution for Mother's death to think much about it.

After today's demonstration, I couldn't sidestep the issue any longer.

Some event—Mother's death?—had yanked the brakes off my magic and catapulted me into a whole new realm. One where I was stronger than any other witch living or dead.

As someone who's always kept to herself, the concept of being thrust into any kind of limelight made me uncomfortable. Yet, if Damien were to be believed, and he had no reason to lie to me, I was some kind of latter day witch queen formed by Hecate to deliver the sisterhood from evil.

I worked automatically, gathering wood and lighting a fire, with my thoughts a tumultuous riot.

Zeke's never been the "I told you so" type. He followed me inside the cabin and curled up near the fire. When I finally settled into a worn leather chair, I wasn't any closer to finding answers.

It had been dark for a couple of hours, and I'd fed my fledgling fire a few times, before I started wondering where

Damien was. His association with me was dangerous for him.

Fae are ancient, but not particularly strong magically.

Had he run into trouble? Did he need my help?

I chewed my lower lip and stared at the rise and fall of the flames. My stomach growled. Zeke had feasted, but my last meal had been the previous day.

"*Want me to hunt you a couple of rabbits?*" Zeke asked sleepily. He must have heard my stomach rumbling.

"Sure. Um, no. I'll live. I'm worried about Damien."

Zeke wasn't quite on his feet, but he'd rolled onto his belly.

"*When did he say he'd be back?*"

"He didn't, but he's been gone maybe fifteen hours. It's a long time."

"*If we leave and he comes here, he'll worry,*" the wolf pointed out.

"I can leave him a note. But my intent is to track him. Means we'd locate him before he returned to this spot."

I stood and walked toward the door.

"*Where are you going?*" If Zeke had been truly concerned, he'd have joined me. His overly full tummy was calling the shots. He'd stand beside me, but only if I needed his protection.

"I'm going to deploy seeking magic. Easier from outdoors."

"*Do not leave without me.*" Zeke curled back into a ball.

"No worries on that front. I'll be in the yard."

I grabbed my coat off a hook and snuggled into it. The evening was chilly, and this way I wouldn't squander magic keeping warm. I passed the bottom step and faced away from the house.

Eyes closed, I sought Damien's unique magical signature. All mages have them. At first, nothing pinged off my casting. Had too many hours passed? Should I have done this midday instead of traipsing off on a carefree hike?

I visualized his six-foot-five-inch height, broad shoulders, and fair hair spilling down his back. Green eyes shaded to moss when he was concerned, and delicate points graced his ears. He was beauty incarnate in a decidedly masculine way. My concern surged to a new level.

Try harder, an inner voice urged.

Duh. What choice did I have? To leave here in search of Damien meant I needed a ballpark idea about where he'd gone. Failing that, I could rattle Faery's gates and see if anyone would show up and let me inside.

Since I'm not Fae, I cannot penetrate the veils separating Fae lands from Earth. At one point, Damien had said he'd see about fixing that problem and allowing me access, but he wouldn't have had time with everything else that's transpired.

Back to "try harder."

I cycled through every element and every direction, experimenting with different combinations. Occasionally, I'd get a faint hit, but it eluded me when I tried to glom onto it.

It finally occurred to me that he'd masked his movements.

Did he not want me following him?

A glance at the stars and half-moon suggested it was

pushing midnight. Waiting here forever wasn't wise. Zeke and I would survive, but I couldn't stand not knowing where Damien was.

I clumped back up the steps. The fire was reduced to a glowing bed of coals. No point in feeding it.

Zeke opened one eye. *"That took a while."*

"Because nothing worked for me."

"Do you want to look for him?"

I nodded. "Problem is where to start. He didn't share his plans."

The wolf got to his feet and shook himself from head to tail tip. *"We can go to Faery. Surely, they have a way of keeping track of their people."*

"I can't get in. Not without Damien or Logan or one of the Fae," I reminded him.

Zeke's tail swished from side to side. *"I can. I'll mind link with Sita."*

"Perfect. Why didn't I think of that?" Bending, I hugged his furry head.

"Because you're not a familiar."

State the obvious, why don't you. Sita was a hawk. She'd been Mother's bird and was devastated by her death. Since she couldn't return to the Coven and witches who'd tortured and killed her bondmate, she'd chosen to remain in Faery.

I took stock of the few things in the cabin. Garments, my notebook, and a few of Damien's magical accoutrements. They'd be safe enough, but I stacked and folded and layered protection spells over everything. Before the spell part, I tore a page out of my notebook and scratched *Looking for you* on it. Those words could mean anything if they were intercepted.

"We're ready," I told the wolf.

He followed me down the steps.

The cottage lacked a lock, so I sealed it with magic. If anyone tried to enter—unlikely since no roads led to this location—they'd encounter a hell of a shock.

After visualizing the place I'd crossed into Faery the times I'd been there, I loosed my spell. Just as before, the transition was so fast it stole my breath. I'd been about to nudge Zeke into action, but he'd already deployed telepathy calling Sita.

Not sure what I'd been expecting, but Maeve and Logan appeared immediately. Sita rode on Maeve's shoulder but made a beeline for Zeke. They'd been friends when Mother and I were still part of the Coven.

"Thanks for coming so quickly," I began.

"Took you long enough," Maeve snapped. One of the Fae seers, she was tall, gaunt, and garbed in a black robe sashed in red. White hair fell to shoulder level, and she skewered me with ice-blue eyes.

"We've been expecting you for hours," Logan added. Head of the Fae council, he was about Maeve's height with gobs of blond curls. Almond-shaped silver eyes stared at me. A blue robe hung off his shoulders, half covering black trousers.

Why oh why do the fucking Fae always put me on the defensive?

"Damien told me to wait for him," I said. "When it grew later and later, I tried to track him and couldn't. So we came here. Why were you expecting me sooner? What do you know? Is Damien all right?"

Once the questions started, I couldn't stem the flow.

Magic glowed around Zeke and Sita as they communicated telepathically.

"Do you suppose it's safe to let her in?" Logan exchanged a pointed glance with Maeve.

Magic began at the crown of my head, scouring me. It burned and stung, but I held still.

"Aye," Maeve replied. "She had naught to do with this."

"With what?" I shouted, sick of them treating me much as the Coven had, like a miscreant and outcast.

Not that I was one of them to begin with, but we'd fought together. Surely, it counted for something. Comrades in arms and all that rot.

"Follow us," Logan instructed.

"Not safe to talk out here," Maeve added.

The veils parted; the Fae stepped through, along with Zeke and Sita. I hesitated, but not for long. If I blew Maeve and Logan off, they'd probably never open Faery to me again.

Seething and worried sick, I plodded through just in time for one of the veils to clip my backside as it fell into place.

"Ouch," I muttered. How could a thing that looked so diaphanous pack such a punch?

"Your own fault," Logan said without looking back.

"Be quicker next time." Piled on the heels of his comment, Maeve's rebuke rankled.

"They know something," Zeke spoke into my mind.

"Tell me something I don't know."

"Means we'll put up with whatever we need to. Damien is in trouble. He needs us."

Faery spread around us. I focused on breathing, just breathing. Unleashing my fury on Damien's people would buy me less than nothing. They'd release information in their own sweet time.

Once I knew more, I'd come up with a plan to fix whatever had gone awry.

The doors to the council chamber closed behind us. The room was large, majestic. Appointed with marble and crystal, thick rugs, an oblong table for the council, and chairs arrayed in rows behind it. To my surprise, the room was full of Fae. Pointed ears quivered with outrage. Almond-shaped eyes glared my way.

Hecate's tits. What the hell was I guilty of?

"Remain standing," Logan ordered.

Zeke took up his position by my side.

Maeve walked close. "Damien has been captured," she said. "By the PDA."

"We tried to free him," Logan snarled. "And failed."

I squared my shoulders, enjoying my better than six-foot height, which made me tower over most of the Fae.

"Tell me where he is. I'll work on it."

"Pfft. Like you can succeed where we failed," Maeve muttered and waved a dismissive hand.

"How about if you don't discount me before I've even left the gate." I held her gaze, not the simplest task.

"Good point," Logan gritted.

I wanted to ask why any of this was my fault, but it

didn't matter. What did was pulling Damien out of the jaws of doom. I had no idea what the PDA did to those they captured, but I'd find out soon enough.

Zeke woofed. His signal we should get moving.

"Are you coming?" I asked Sita.

The hawk quorked and ruffled her feathers.

"Tell me where he is," I repeated. "So I can get moving."

"We don't like it he selected you as his mate," Logan said, "but, in this instance, it might work to our advantage."

My mouth flapped open. I shut it fast.

Mate? What the fuck?

Zeke nudged me. In my confusion, I'd missed Maeve's instructions.

"Never mind, I have them," the wolf said and gripped my lower arm in his jaws.

Together, we walked out of the chamber and retraced our steps, intent on leaving Faery.

"Where are we going?" I asked Zeke.

A series of images spilled through my mind. My mouth split in half a grin. At least the first part would be straightforward. Best not get too cocky.

Who knew what we'd find in an ironclad compound beneath Seattle's waterfront. To be on the safe side, I put out a call to the Mer people as I loosed my teleport spell. My first stop would be their domain for reinforcements. With witches' affinity for the natural world, we've always gotten along well with sea-dwellers.

Like me, they're not sensitive to iron, and the Fae are their allies.

At least I believed they were. Begged the question why

Logan and Maeve hadn't thought to request aid from that quarter.

Much like my earlier question about what the PDA did to their captives, this one would find an answer sooner rather than later.

Water closed around us as my spell brought us to the Mer people's castle a few hundred yards out to sea. I switched to drawing oxygen from water rather than air and surrounded Zeke and Sita in a bubble.

A glittering shell and stone structure was right in front of me. Lights flickered from several windows courtesy of specialized reflective lichen. I raised a hand and knocked.

"No witches," filtered from somewhere within.

Oh-oh. Word of the Coven's association with evil must have spread.

I can breathe underwater, but I can't speak, not out loud. *"But I'm one of the good ones,"* I protested. *"Hecate chose me."*

The door flew open. A lissome mermaid with aqua scales, matching eyes, long golden hair, and bare breasts examined me.

"So the olden tales are true?"

I nodded. No one had educated me about any "olden tales" regarding Hecate and her plans, but bringing it up would muddy the waters. *"They are, and I've come for your aid."*

For the second time in an hour, magic analyzed me, cutting deep. I must have passed because the mermaid swam aside, gesturing me in. I ushered the bubble containing Zeke and Sita alongside me. We couldn't remain long; I'd have to be damned convincing pleading my case.

"Are you certain you don't want to send them back to the shore?" The mermaid arched fair brows.

I shook my head. *"Someone has it in for me. They're not safe. Neither am I."*

"I see. Hurry, then. Follow me."

CHAPTER TWO, DAMIEN

My first mistake was returning to the boardinghouse. I wanted to make damn good and certain I'd eradicated any evidence of me having been there. I'd done a decent job wiping the slate clear of Morgan's magic, but had neglected my own.

After the bloodbath in the street and the dead witches, someone was bound to go through the building with a fine-toothed comb.

I might have gotten away with being sloppy. Almost did. I'd finished my room and was sprinkling neutralizing spells throughout the building when two burly shifters appeared out of nowhere and stopped me in the upstairs hall.

My second mistake was not teleporting the fuck out of there immediately.

"Fae, eh?" one growled. He was tall and burly with coal black hair, blue eyes, and a full beard. His khaki uniform sported a runic emblem above the PDA initials. The outline of a wolf formed behind him.

I nodded pleasantly. "Aye. But I pass as mortal. Work construction in West Seattle."

"Why?" the other sneered. Half a foot shorter than his companion, he sported brown curls, dark eyes, and was smooth shaven. Garbed in an identical uniform, a fox formed behind him. "Did they kick your sorry ass out of Underhill?"

"We call it Faery, and no, my status with my kinsmen hasn't been tarnished."

"Why?" the wolf repeated his comrade. "No mage in their right mind chooses Earth over a magical land."

"You did," I pointed out.

He shook his head. "Not the same. Shifters don't have our own world."

"The work I did for my people was unappreciated, so I took a slight hiatus about thirty years back."

"What kind of work was that?" The fox narrowed his eyes.

"I got a jump on black magic wielders before they could breach our borders. And I kept supplies flowing. It grew more difficult in the modern world. Not so simple to divert a goat or a cow anymore without someone noticing they were gone."

Offering a complicit smile, I layered believability around me. Mostly, I wanted these two clowns to get lost, so I could return to the important stuff: finding a temporary home for Morgan and me.

And Zeke and Sita.

Magic flickered between the shifters. They were talking. I tried to listen in, but couldn't. Fae magic isn't particularly robust, but I'd have thought it sufficient to intercept mind speech between two shifters.

"How long have you lived here?" the wolf asked..

"A few months."

"Know anything about the shitshow out there?" The fox jerked a thumb in the general direction of the front of the building.

I shook my head. "What shitshow?" Turning, I started for the fire escape, intent on looking outside.

"Not so fast." The wolf grabbed my arm.

I tried to shake him off. Ha. May as well have been chained to a boulder.

"I was going to look outside," I protested. "You mentioned a problem."

Magic scrabbled at the edges of my mind. I'd wisely dropped a ward into place, and I cemented the edges.

"We think you know something," the fox proclaimed.

I stared him down. "Well, I don't." I made shooing motions with both hands. "Don't the two of you have a job to do?"

"Yeah, and it's right here," the wolf growled.

Oh-oh.

I activated my emergency link with Faery and hoped to hell someone was paying attention. I'd only resorted to this Draconian move a few times before.

Once, it had actually worked.

And then I made a grab for a journey spell. I hadn't

expected it to come together, and it didn't. A wedge sat between me and my magic.

The wolf still had hold of my arm. The fox stood on my other side.

"You're under arrest," he declared. Iron cuffs flickered into view. He snapped one into place around the nearest wrist.

"For what?" Fury roared through me.

"Withholding knowledge," the wolf sneered.

I'd already told them I knew nothing. They hadn't believed me. More words wouldn't change it.

"What about my rights?" I demanded.

"Mages don't have rights," the fox informed me. "Where the fuck have you been, dude? Under a dumpster?"

I jerked the handcuffs out of his grasp and swatted him across the face. The iron cut deep; blood welled, dripping down his cheekbone.

Mistake number three.

The wolf twisted my arm behind my back, got hold of the loose cuff, and did his damnedest to muscle me into submission.

I fought back. My skill was slow to respond, but I drove one wave of defensive magic after another into the shifters. No longer human, they'd turned into their respective animals.

Fuck.

Now I had teeth and claws to contend with.

If anyone in Faery had picked up on my distress call, they weren't in a hurry to ride to the rescue. I'd remember that—if I ever got back there.

I had to get out of this mess. Had to. Morgan and Zeke were waiting for me. What would they do if I didn't return?

I cut that line of thought off at the roots.

Morgan was resourceful and stronger than me when it came to raw ability. She'd know something had intervened to delay me. We were practically betrothed. Not that I'd come out and asked her to be my mate, but I'd shared my intentions with Maeve. So my kin wouldn't be blindsided by my plans to wed outside the blood.

Oberon's balls, my mind was wandering. I needed to be present. Right here. Right now.

The wolf had his jaws around my calf. I'd beat him back with magic, so the damage wasn't great. Not yet. The fox clung to my shoulders, doing his damnedest to close his puny jaws around my neck where he could do some real harm.

Not a battle I could win. Eventually, they'd overpower me, and I'd be screwed. Imprisoned and injured. Better to cut my losses. I needed all my strength to escape from wherever they dumped me.

"Stop," I thundered. "I'll go with you."

The wolf took his sweet time shifting back. "Why would you agree if you're not guilty as sin?"

"To avoid the two of you tearing holes in me." I spread my hands in front of me. "Just so we're clear. I am not guilty of anything beyond living here. And I'm actually in the process of moving out. If you check with the foreman at my jobsite, he'll tell you I quit yesterday morning."

"Moving where?" The fox was back to his man form.

"Back to Faery. The council will verify."

"Thought you had a falling out with them." The wolf growled.

"Thirty years back, yeah. We have a common enemy, and we've closed ranks."

"Oh really?" The fox sounded intrigued. "Who?"

"Not at liberty to say."

A high-pitched whistling sound emerged from the fox. "We're wasting time."

"Let's move him out of here," the wolf agreed. "Then we can return and search for clues."

Thank the goddess no trace of Morgan remained. Wolves and foxes are exceptional trackers.

Unfamiliar magic circled me. They still hadn't clipped the other cuff into place. I chose not to remind them of their oversight. Keeping my hands at my sides, I hung onto the dangling cuff so it wouldn't make noise.

The upstairs hall dropped away, replaced by a circular chamber lined with bricks. No windows. My bet was we were underground. A sink and toilet sat off to one side. The floor was dirt. The opposite side of the space held a gallon container that might have been full of water.

Before I had a chance to ask questions, the two PDA agents left. Their portal winked out behind them. I took stock of my body. Other than a couple of sore spots, no one's teeth had broken my skin. The handcuff was a problem, but it would have been worse if my hands were cuffed together.

May as well be methodical about this. My first move was exploring just how much magic I had access to.

Answer: none. Or not enough to do anything meaningful, so it may as well have been none.

Next, I walked the circular perimeter of my prison. Didn't take long to determine the bricks had been laid over a continuous sheet of plate steel. No reason to even attempt telepathy. No one would hear me.

I sniffed the water jug when I drew near. Stale, but not poisoned. I took a tentative sip to see if it had been spelled.

Nope.

Just water.

If mages had no rights, did it mean we also didn't get fed? Time would tell on that front.

At least my cell was dry. I sat cross-legged near the center as far from the plate steel as I could get and contemplated my options.

Much as I hated to admit it, there weren't any.

Or were there?

I've always had an affinity for earth. Plenty of that beneath my feet. I might not be able to drill through the sides, and the ceiling was a million feet above my head, but escape through the floor was a possibility.

I lay on my belly, ear flattened to the ground, and sent tentacles of seeking enchantment downward. They didn't bounce back and slap me. Encouraged, I called softly for the earth goddess, making certain what remained of my magic —and my voice—traveled in a single direction: downward.

Cold seeped into me. I persevered.

Asking for help isn't in my wheelhouse. It's demeaning when I can't solve my own problems. Activating my emergency linkage with Faery had been a blow to my pride.

I'd done it anyway.

Here I was, hat in hand, groveling. No choice. It wasn't

as if I could dig myself out of here. Even if my ability suddenly scaled to 100 percent, I'd still have hell's own time moving enough dirt to tunnel to freedom.

"What is it?" A sleepy, annoyed voice padded across my mind.

I'd had a bunch of flowery words prepared. I junked them. *"Trapped. Need help."*

"Why me?"

"I cannot do this by myself."

Arrgh. Just shoot me now. Nothing quite like admitting failure—and to a goddess, no less.

"Why not?"

"Surrounded by iron. Please. The Fae would be forever grateful, and—"

"They already are." She didn't sound nearly as sleepy.

"Name your price."

"Not sure I have one."

Unfamiliar magic was closing on me. Must be the shifters, or some other sanctimonious PDA bastards come to check on their latest acquisition.

"Hurry," I urged. *"Or it will be too late."*

Voices and footsteps grew louder. Of course, this enclosure would have a door somewhere, even if I hadn't located one. It wasn't efficient to maintain a prison where the only way in or out required expenditure of magic.

With zero warning, I was yanked downward. Dirt barely opened to allow my passage. The hole above me closed blanking out all light. Outraged shrieks followed my descent until I couldn't hear them any longer.

I'd cut my egress far too close.

The iron cuff still dangled from one wrist.

"What is that abomination?" The goddess's voice boomed around me. My wrist caught fire before the snap of metal told me she'd burned through the offending circlet. The stench of burning flesh—mine—stung my nostrils.

To avoid inhaling dust and dirt particles, I kept my breaths shallow, but singed flesh has its own icky odor.

The downward journey took a long time.

Suddenly, the dirt that dragged at me turned into salt water.

I was free; the goddess was gone.

Breathing underwater is second nature, but I got a lungful before I made the transition. My body would absorb it.

I reached for my ability, relief spilling through me when it bounded to my command.

Without preamble, I set a course for Faery. The PDA couldn't follow me there. They'd be a problem, but only if I got frisky and wasn't careful watching my back.

Ha. Total understatement. Leaving Faery wasn't in my immediate future. Not unless I was warded to within an inch of my existence.

I could do that, but it would burn through scads of magic.

I'd have to plan my outings carefully. A safe haven for Morgan and me might end up being in Faery for a while.

At least until things cooled down.

In all my years living amongst men, it never occurred to me I'd become a target. Why had the two agents zeroed in on me?

I'd toss it out to the council. Many minds were always better than mine alone.

Faery took shape around me, and then I came to my senses. My first stop should have been the cabin in the South Cascades to gather Morgan and Zeke.

Keeping my portal active, I layered so many wards around myself not even my best friends—if I had any— would recognize me.

Satisfied, I set a course for the cabin. I wouldn't stay long.

The velvet of a mountain night surrounded me as I emerged in front of the humble structure. I bounded up the steps and opened the door.

Empty.

No one was here. I reached with magic, scattering it wide, to confirm my findings.

The dregs of a fire suggested Morgan had left hours ago.

Damn it.

A scrap of paper beckoned. I opened it to read, *Looking for you.*

I'd hoped she'd have at least waited until tomorrow morning.

She hadn't.

I flicked my fingers, eradicating evidence of all of us from this place. I'd tap Logan, or one of my other kinsmen, to return to the cabin and track where Morgan had gone.

I could have done it, but I'd have had to jettison my wards. If I were captured again, they'd never let me escape. Worry dogged me as I returned to Faery. Along with a sense of helplessness, which rankled. The fucking PDA had me over a barrel.

If they captured Morgan, I'd burn the bloody world down and make every agent sorry they'd ever been born. Or hatched. Or made.

For the second time in half an hour, Faery's soothing presence surrounded me. I pounded down corridors, intent on the central meeting area.

I'd get to the bottom of this mess, but I had to move fast. Morgan had been through enough. I'd promised to keep her safe.

So far, I'd done a piss-poor job, but that was about to change.

CHAPTER THREE, MORGAN

The Mer people have always been a chatty lot, but I didn't have time to spare. To avoid appearing rude, I gestured toward the familiars suspended in their bubble of air.

The mermaid who'd let me in cupped her hands around her rose-petal mouth, projecting her voice through the castle. "We must listen to the witch before her creatures run out of breathing space."

A throng swam into view.

"Thank you." I glanced at a collection of male and female Mer people with hair in a rainbow of colors and scales ranging from deep blue to pale green.

No reason to wait until everyone arrived. I dove right in. *"Damien, one of the Fae, has been captured by the PDA."*

A cacophony of hisses filled the water with bubbles.

"He is in an ironclad prison beneath the Seattle waterfront."

"Aye, we know it too well," the mermaid said.

"Can we free him?" I asked.

Power sparked, turning the water crystalline as the Mer folk conversed amongst one another.

"Meet us on shore at Pier 60." The mermaid swished her tail. "There is a peephole beneath the dock. We will look inside and plan from there."

"How can we see through iron?"

One of the males laughed uproariously. "We drilled a small hole. So far, no one has noticed."

"Your Fae is scarcely the first to be targeted," another mermaid said.

Fascinating. When Damien had told me about the PDA, I hadn't taken them seriously. Bunch of two-bit mages playing god for mortals. Apparently, I'd underestimated their reach. The topic had never come up in the Coven, likely because none of us ever left there for long.

"I'll wait for you at the pier," I told them.

"Under the pier," the mermaid clarified. "Where no one will see you."

"Thank you all very much." I inclined my head and crafted a journey spell. My aim wasn't perfect since this area wasn't all that familiar to me. I ended up maybe a quarter mile away, but covered the distance quickly while encouraging my garments to dry.

Sita rode on my shoulder. Zeke, wearing the dog glamour I'd created for him, trotted by my side. We passed a few down-at-the-heels humans who eyed us as if we were fresh meat to carve.

Until Zeke showed his fangs, growling menacingly.

"Thanks," I murmured.

He rubbed his damp, furry head against my thigh.

Pier 60 turned out to be the Seattle Aquarium and an entrance to the famous Public Market. It was crawling with people. Many eyed me oddly. Between my still-soggy clothes and my animal honor guard, I must have looked like one of the street people who'd creeped me out.

The dock extended into the bay. A chain stretched across it with warning signs not to cross beyond its length.

The only way I'd finesse getting beneath it would be to cloak all of us in invisibility. Where to manage it was the challenge. I couldn't wink out of sight in the midst of a throng. Well, I could, but it wouldn't be wise.

Someone might call the PDA.

With the prevalence of cell phone cameras, one of the many people giving me a wide berth had probably already snapped a picture. If not, surveillance cameras had done it for them.

I could just hear the discourse: "Officer. One minute, this sketchy looking woman with a dog and a bird was right here, but then she vanished. No, I haven't been drinking. Everyone else saw the same thing."

I crossed the street to a parking lot intending to crouch between cars to accomplish my task. Except I couldn't get fully out of sight. Damn it. The Mer people were probably waiting for us.

They'd done me a favor. It was rude to hold them up.

A good-sized motorhome chugged into the lot and took up three spaces. A family poured out its side door, three children racing toward the flashing aquarium sign. A couple followed, yelling at their spawn to slow down. Was anyone else in the vehicle?

I risked a scan.

Empty. Perfect for my needs. I gave the family sufficient time to cross the wide boulevard and let myself into their home, slapping don't-look-here spells around us as I mounted the stairs with Zeke and Sita.

"Bold," Zeke commented.

"More like desperate. Hush now. Couple of minutes and we'll be gone."

With the innate wisdom of birds, Sita remained silent.

I can be quick, and, with my newly augmented ability, it didn't take more than a minute for me to wrap us in invisibility and transport us beneath the dock. The Mer people were indeed waiting. Three of them. The water was dank and oily. It smelled of decayed fish and fuel from ships.

"What took you so long?" the mermaid who'd let me into the castle asked.

"Sorry. Miscalculations on my part." Ducking my head until my eyes were even with water level, I saw the peephole.

"Don't bother," a male Mer person with long copper hair and blue eyes said. "The cell is empty."

"Aye, your friend was there," the mermaid added. "We sense his energy, but he found a way out."

Breath whooshed from me. "Are you certain the PDA didn't move him?"

"Quite," the male said. "When we arrived, several of them were milling about the cell cursing."

The third Mer person was a woman with violet hair and

matching eyes. "Aye, they were furious their quarry had escaped and were planning to broadcast his picture over every police network."

"They said he's wanted for killing five women." The first mermaid focused her attention squarely on me. "Is it true?"

I swallowed hard. No place for anything except the truth. "It was five witches, the bad kind," I clarified. "And I killed them."

"How?" the second mermaid asked. "Isn't your kind immortal?"

"Yes, we are. As to the other, I can't answer that," I admitted. "I only meant to punish them for stalking me after they kicked me out of the Coven. They were scattering hex bags around my residence, and I was worried innocents would be harmed."

Three sets of eyes stared at me. Zeke treaded water by my side. Sita remained on my shoulder.

"So, what happened?" the first mermaid asked.

I gripped the edge of the pier. "Something shifted in my ability. It got stronger. A lot stronger. Damien did his best to call me back, but the damage was already done. I'm not sorry they're dead, but I'd rather not have been the instrument of their destruction."

"We'd heard all witches signed a pact with the Fuath," the first mermaid said.

Fuath, huh? They were a loosely established band of evil spirits roaming the Highlands.

"And Kelpies," the merman tossed out.

I shook my head. "I know about a pact with darkness, but it can't be all witches. Fuath are a long way from here.

Hard to see how they'd be part of anything on this side of the Atlantic."

I started to explain what I knew about Kelpies, but it was so obscure and complicated I saved my breath.

"It does seem remote," the merman agreed.

"Certainly, some witches are implicated," I went on. "They captured my mother and tortured and killed her to ensure she couldn't tell me anything about my origins."

"What does Hecate have to say about all this?" the second mermaid asked.

"I have no idea. One of my tasks is to locate her. So far, I haven't had time to do anything except defend myself."

"Time to get on with finding her," the merman said. "Nothing more for you to attend to here since the Fae extricated himself."

"I need to talk with Damien before I go anywhere," I murmured. "He's probably in Faery, except I have no way to get inside."

"Stand by the gates like you did last time," Zeke suggested.

The filthy water was sinking into my bones, chilling me to my core. "Thank you so much for your help," I told the Mer people.

"We have always been allies with the Fae." The violet-haired mermaid smiled.

"Aye, give them our best," the male added.

The group flipped their tails around and swam into the bay. The pollution didn't appear to affect them, but it was taking a toll on me.

Time to leave.

By now Damien had probably been back to the cabin. He

would have found my note, but he'd be worried sick about me. Unless he'd stopped by Faery. If he did, someone would tell him I'd been there and was still in one piece.

I gathered power into an arc and aimed for the gateway into Faery. If I got lucky, someone would be watching for me and open the veils. The murky water ceded first to darkness and then to the place I'd stood before hoping for entrance.

"That water was nasty." Zeke shook himself. Might have helped him, but all it did was soak me with more of the noxious stuff.

I wrapped my arms around myself and directed a flow of magic to keep warm. Our last visit, Sita had been in Faery, and Zeke had alerted her we stood at the gates. This time, she was with us and uncharacteristically quiet. If his telepathy worked from this vantage point, mine should too.

Who to call?

May as well start with Damien. Maybe I'd get lucky. I raised my mind voice. His name had no sooner left my thoughts than he catapulted through the veils and snatched me into his arms.

His lips smashed into mine. Desperation ran through the kiss and his touch. Almost as if he'd been afraid he'd never see me again.

It felt good in his arms with his mouth over mine. Too good. I kissed him back with such fervor it was like some other woman stood here. Heat coursed through me, cutting the chill from my soaking wet garments.

How could he have such an effect on me where we became the only two beings in the world? I couldn't imagine not standing here with his mouth over mine, teasing his tongue with my own.

Sita cooed softly. Zeke leaned against my legs, yipping happily.

"Christ, woman." Damien ripped his mouth away, still cradling my head in one hand and placing the other on my waist. "I was so worried when you weren't at the cabin. I got the note, but why'd you leave so soon?"

"You were gone for hours," I protested, voice raspy with passion.

"Damn it. You're soaked. Where have you been?" He loosened his hold enough to look at me.

"Hunting for you. Where else?"

"Aw, sweetheart." He shook his head. "What am I doing. Come into Faery. Let's get you into some dry clothes that don't smell like ocean sludge."

Part of me—a damned big part—could have cared less about being dry. What I wanted was more kissing. More of his body pressed against mine with the tantalizing bulge that jutted into my stomach.

"Food?" Zeke woofed hopefully.

Damien ruffled the fur on his head. "Could be arranged, mate."

"I'm hungry too," Sita announced. Her vocal cord arrangement supports speech. Zeke's doesn't.

"All the more reason to come within."

Damien barked a few words in Gaelic. The veils parted, and we hustled through.

"Can you find the wardrobe room again?" he asked.

I nodded.

"Excellent. I'll see to getting these two fed. Meet you in the council chamber."

Before I walked two feet away, Maeve bustled up. "You're back. From the looks of you, you paid a visit to the Mer people. How are they?"

"Let her change before you interrogate her," Damien cut in. By my side again, he placed a protective arm around my shoulders. The Coven-me would have protested. This version craved his solicitousness.

She cast a sidelong glance his way. "Weren't you on your way to do something?"

I leaned into him. "We'll be fine. See you soon."

"I want to hear about where you've been too, but it will keep." He kissed my cheek before herding the wolf and hawk down one of many corridors.

Maeve waited until we were inside the Fae's spacious wardrobe chamber before asking after the Mer people again. She also requested a rundown of my activities.

I'd been in this place before. Women's garments ranged along one side, men's the other. Apparently, someone had been collecting clothing since before the Middle Ages.

I went to the far right side where modern clothing resided in armoires, cupboards, and drawers. Stripping off my still-sodden garments, I hung them on hooks. Before I left, I'd run them through a magic-infused washing machine.

I'd begun layering a green woolen tunic over soft, black pants when I stopped long enough to address her questions. "It's pretty simple," I told Maeve. "My first stop was the Mer people. You'd told me Damien was held captive in an underwater lair, so they were a logical choice.

"At first, they didn't want to let me inside their dwelling. Witches' reputations have fallen on hard times. I had to convince them I was one of the good ones."

I paused to take a breath and pull a warm multicolored jacket over the tunic. "They'd heard rumors about Hecate creating me." I shook my head and sat on a bench to smooth dry socks over my feet. "Seems as if everyone knew about me, except me."

"Did they say anything about the Fae?" Maeve persisted.

I cocked my head to one side, remembering. "Only that you were allies."

Breath swooshed from her. "Good. Means they aren't holding a grudge."

"About what?" I looked up from tying my boots.

"None of your affair."

I stared at her. All right, then. Acceptance only went so far.

Careful to hold my tongue, I moved my discarded clothes to the magic-imbued cleaning apparatus and waited a few moments for them to move through its laser-driven cycle.

When they were done, I draped them over my arm. "Damien said to meet in the council chamber. Is there a gathering? Or was it just a convenient spot to catch up with one another?"

"A little of both. Damien is a wanted man. He won't be able to poke his nose outside Faery for a good long time."

She didn't tack on that his problems were my fault, but

she may as well have. I saw her thoughts clearly because she didn't bother to cloak them.

"I'm appreciative for everything you've done for me," I murmured as we walked out of the wardrobe chamber.

"You should be. You don't have anywhere else to go."

My temper has never been my long suit, and it finally reared up in outrage. I stopped dead. "I'd figure something out. I always have. Why don't you like me?"

She held up a hand and counted off on her fingers. "One. You're not Fae. Two. Trouble follows you like a magnet." Three. "Because you're in Faery, that trouble has become our problem."

"Fine. I'll take my wolf and go." Racing ahead, I put distance between the dour mage and myself.

She caught up easily and curved a hand around my arm. I tugged to escape, but she held fast. "Not so fast, missy. It's not as simple as you walking out Faery's gates. Your fate is inextricably twined with ours. I have yet to see the full story, but enough snatches have come through to convince me we're stuck with you.

"And then there's the small ripple that one of ours loves you. Fae rarely mate—"

"You're going on as if it's a done deal," I sputtered. "Damien and I scarcely know one another. I can't predict where our futures will lead."

"I can. Now, come on. People are waiting for us."

I trudged next to Maeve, my thoughts a jumble. I had to locate Hecate. I didn't have space for much else in my life. Who knew how the witch goddess would react to her long lost minion.

Maybe she wouldn't want anything to do with me. Perhaps her plans, hatched centuries ago, had changed and no longer included me.

Regardless, I had to find out.

Damien wasn't any part of it. Maeve had pointed out he was a wanted man and couldn't leave Faery. I could, and I would just as soon as the meeting someone had planned about me without consulting me was over.

CHAPTER FOUR, DAMIEN

While the animals fed and the wolf cleaned up, I considered what to do next. Logan and the others had made it clear I wasn't to leave Faery, not for a good long while.

We'd see about it.

I couldn't help Morgan from behind Faery's veils. And I would not allow her to set off on her own. No way was I repeating the hell I'd gone through when I couldn't find her and had no idea where to look.

Good luck with that, mate, an inner voice piped up. Morgan was her own witch. She wouldn't react well to edicts flowing from my lips.

The council wouldn't hold me prisoner. Well, they could, but they wouldn't. I'd done nothing wrong. I'd taken plenty of risks during the years I'd spied for my people. The difference was no one had known about them except me.

And the PDA weren't involved, the same inner voice chimed in.

Crap. Why hadn't I gotten the fuck out of the boardinghouse before things heated up?

Because never in my wildest imaginings did I expect those two shifters to shanghai me.

Great. I was answering myself. Enough of this.

Zeke was polishing off the last of a cow femur. The mice I'd fed Sita were long gone.

"Ready to get moving?" I asked.

Zeke woofed; Sita cawed.

I herded them uphill toward the council chamber, enjoying their presence. The Fae have never bonded with animals. Not because we couldn't; it never occurred to us.

"Glad you're okay," Zeke told me.

"Me too," Sita chirped.

"Could have been worse." I aimed for a chipper note. Yeah, it could have been so much worse. I could still be in that metal-lined chamber at the mercy of the PDA and whatever they did to captives.

I had a feeling it wasn't pretty.

We walked through tall double doors leading into the council chamber. It was filled to bursting with Fae.

Of course it was. Nothing much interesting ever happened in Faery.

Morgan ran to us. Garbed in dry clothes, she was striking with thick, shiny dark hair falling to the middle of her back, stark bone structure, and mismatched eyes, one brown, the other white. She's tall, around six feet, and slender. Full breasts pushed against a stretchy top. A jacket hung off her shoulders. Her narrow waist was encased in dark trousers that flowed over flared hips and down her long legs. Stout lace-up scuffed leather boots graced her feet.

Zeke placed his paws on her shoulders. She hugged him before saying, "Ewww, you're still wet."

"Takes a while," he reminded her and licked her mouth before retreating to the floor.

"I know. My Pier 60 clothes are hanging over that chair." She pointed.

Chimes rippled through the generous room with its large oblong wooden table for the council members and gallery seating for everyone else. Multiple conversations quieted.

I led my small contingent to the left side of the room and waited while Morgan settled into a padded chair. I sat next to her with Sita on my shoulder. Zeke curled on the floor between us, but he was only pretending to be asleep. Tension radiated from Morgan's familiar. He'd defend her to the death if anyone so much as looked cross-eyed at her.

Logan stood at the head of the table, waiting for everyone's full attention.

"Thank you all for coming," he said. "We have decisions to make today. For the first time ever, one of our own has come to the attention of the Paranormal Detective Agency—"

"First time in maybe twenty years," someone called from the rear of the room. "PDA's not much older than that."

Logan glared at the Fae who'd spoken. When I zeroed in on him, I wasn't surprised to identify Ramon. He'd never been one for following rules and had been vocal about the PDA being a bunch of cowards hiding behind mortals' skirts.

"Silence until I request comments." Logan's tone could have etched glass. "If anyone cannot contain themselves, the door is that way." He extended an arm. His robe, black today sashed in gold, billowed around him. His pointed ears quivered with annoyance.

"This is ridiculous," Ramon muttered loud enough for the entire room to hear before he turned on his heel and left.

"Does anyone wish to join him?" Logan asked in a neutral voice that probably masked fury.

We all have our roles for good reasons. Logan is a decent leader, but he doesn't tolerate disagreement. Usually, meetings like this were convened so he could tell us what to do.

Not going to happen today. Morgan's independent as hell. I'm none too compliant myself.

No one stirred.

Power shimmered around Logan as he sealed the doors. Not that one of us couldn't leave if we chose, but there'd be no sneaking out.

"Today's meeting is about the witch," Logan went on.

"I have a name." Morgan spoke crisply.

"The rule about not interrupting applies to you too," Logan snarked.

I made a grab for her, but she sprang to her feet, pushing past me into the aisle. Morgan crossed her arms beneath her breasts and glared at Logan.

He stared back. "You can wait outside," he suggested. "We'll let you know what we decide about you."

I winced. This wouldn't end well.

Zeke apparently came to the same conclusion because he stood by Morgan's side, hackles at half-mast.

"You called a meeting about me without consulting me." Morgan's clear, ringing voice filled the room. "While I am sorry Damien ran into difficulties on my account, I have a task to fulfill. Regardless of what transpires today, I'm still leaving as soon as the meeting is over. You cannot stop me. You do not hold jurisdiction over witches."

Maeve shot to her feet, forming an odd triumvirate. "You cannot go by yourself," the Fae seer announced.

"I'll have Zeke with me," Morgan replied.

"It won't be enough," Maeve argued.

"What have you seen?" Logan broke into the conversation that had slipped his control.

"Enough. The witch—"

"I have a name." Morgan repeated her earlier comment. The stubborn tilt to her jaw said she wasn't about to back down.

"Fine," Maeve sputtered, tightlipped. "Morgan will walk into danger the moment she leaves Faery. If she remains, she will bring darkness into our midst. We cannot allow it to happen. No one evil has ever breached Faery's borders."

"So it's better for you if Zeke and I leave," Morgan cut in.

"I'm coming," Sita cawed and scribed circles around the room before landing on Morgan's shoulders.

"What have you seen?" Morgan asked the seer.

"I'm not at liberty to disclose that." She tossed her head.

"Why?"

"You're not Fae."

Fuck this crap. I was on my feet too. "Then tell me," I growled.

Maeve shook her head. "If I do, you'll just tell the wit—, er Morgan. If she follows through on her stated path and leaves, the information could be tortured out of her."

"Thanks for the vote of confidence," Morgan muttered.

I joined Morgan, Zeke, and Sita but addressed my words to Logan. "Either we're all in this together"—I spread my hands in front of me—"or we're not. Morgan's fate is linked with mine. If Maeve knows something, she must reveal what she's seen."

"Aye, Morgan's fate is indeed linked to Faery—and to you." Maeve didn't wait for Logan to order her to speak. Not that it would have made a shred of difference. Despite Logan's delusions of control, no one takes orders well in Faery. It's amazing we've won the battles we fought.

I spun one hand in a get-on-with-it gesture.

Maeve set her mouth in a firm line and didn't say a word.

"I say we let her leave," someone shouted from the gallery.

The chant was taken up through the chamber. I stared at Fae I'd known for hundreds of years, shocked by their level of animosity. None of them knew Morgan, but they'd identified her as an outsider, a threat to Faery's peace.

The chimes sounded again, louder this time and discordant. Silence returned. "I opened this meeting to all of Faery as a courtesy," Logan snapped. "I can limit it to our council, and I will if there is one more outburst."

Spots of color blotched Morgan's cheeks. She was

holding it together by a thread. I knew her well enough to understand she wanted to tell the entire room to fuck off. Arms swinging by her sides, she moved closer to Logan.

"We fought together when you helped rescue Mother in the Old Country. I could have returned with Maeve and Mother. Instead, I remained to ensure you and Damien escaped Banshees and the Dearg."

Logan opened his mouth, but she held up a hand. "I'm not finished. When Zeke and I arrived here and you told me Damien was being held prisoner and you couldn't reach him, I left immediately. He ended up freeing himself, but my intentions were sound.

"I have acted in good faith, and I fail to understand why you're treating me like yesterday's trash."

Zeke woofed for emphasis, tail pluming, ears tucked back. Sita cawed stridently from her perch on Morgan's shoulders.

An undercurrent in her tone chopped holes in my heart. Morgan had been abandoned by her Coven, the only home she'd ever known. Undaunted, she'd set about forging a new life for herself and Zeke. I'd done my damnedest to support her, help her find her way in a world that had to be alien outside the Coven's protected walls.

And now my people were acting the same way as the Coven, labeling Morgan an outsider.

"'Tisn't about you, child," Maeve said.

Morgan focused on the seer. "Oh really? If not me, then whom?"

"The balance that has held Faery apart from events on Earth is threatened," Maeve explained. "I have seen this coming for a long while, but the instrument of change eluded me. Until you showed up. Even now, I'm still putting pieces together."

The pain I felt for Morgan ran through me like a hot tide. "Faery can remain aloof like it always has. I will accompany Morgan and the animals. No need to dirty your hands."

I stopped there. After all I'd done in service to my people, their attitude was crap. Nothing ever remains the same. If Maeve was correct—and she had a stellar track record—change was upon us. We'd do well to roll with the flow rather than stick our heads in the sand.

"You cannot leave," Logan thundered.

"I beg your pardon?" I positioned myself between him and Morgan. "You cannot control where I go nor what I do."

He shook a finger at me. "They will be looking for you. Traps will be everywhere. If they capture you again—"

"They won't." I spoke over him.

Morgan poked me in the back. "Gosh, they don't think much of either of us. I get why your people would underestimate me, but they know you."

Out of the mouths of witches.

The doors at the rear of the chamber flew open. "Everyone but council out of here," Logan barked.

Amidst grumbling, no doubt at losing access to the most entertaining event they'd witnessed in eons, Fae rose and trudged from the room.

"Told you it was a mistake to invite everyone," Maeve groused.

The doors banged shut. Logan didn't bother to seal them. Other than the odd Fae like Ramon, who'd already left, no one wanted a confrontation with Logan. Power flickered around him as he communicated telepathically with someone, probably Maeve.

The seer nodded crisply and addressed her next words to Morgan. "You plan to go after Hecate."

Morgan's eyebrows shot up. "How would you know?"

"Did you really just ask that?"

Morgan flapped a hand her way. "No. Probably not. You must have seen it the same way Lilith saw things in her glass and her pool."

My mind tracked back to a vision Maeve had shared. Lilith was the seer in Morgan's ex-Coven. The witch possessed shapeshifting abilities and morphed into something like Medusa when the sisterhood questioned her.

"I saw parts," Maeve corrected her. "What I have gleaned is far from positive. Locating any of the Greek gods will be fraught with danger. If Hecate meant to follow through with her plans for you, she would have shown up long since."

Maeve blew out a breath. "I fear you're embarking on a fool's errand, one that may cost you dearly."

Zeke growled.

The seer eyed him. "We're on the same side, buddy. I'm trying to protect your mistress."

Morgan dropped a hand on his head, winding her fingers in his fur.

"What else have you seen?" she asked.

"Fires. Earthquakes. Darkness heretofore on the sidelines taking center stage."

"Okay. Why do you believe those things are happening on account of me?" Morgan stood tall, shoulders back, ready to bear whatever burden was tossed her way.

Pride for her swelled through me.

"You're the only element that changed," Maeve replied.

Morgan shook her head. "Not true. My Coven slid off the rails. Witches only used to practice white magic. Many of my former sisters are now fully embroiled in sorcery. They parleyed with the Dearg and Banshees who imprisoned Mother. Kelpies too. Something is afoot. I may be in the eye of the storm, but I do not believe I caused it."

"If you know more, tell us," I pleaded. "Information is power, and right now we don't know all that much."

"You're determined to go with her?" Logan broke in.

I nodded.

Morgan prodded me again. "You don't have to."

I turned to gaze at her standing proud like an ancient queen. "I want to. Our futures are twined."

"Aye, that they are," Maeve agreed.

"Not seeing it." Morgan shook her head. "If what comes next is that dangerous, I should face it alone."

"Not a chance," I told her and refocused on Maeve. "If there's more and you choose to hold it close, you're doing us a disservice."

Maeve shut her eyes. Perhaps she sought guidance from the source of her visions. Finally, she opened them. "If both of you insist on this path, I would see you mated afore you set out. It will strengthen your link, one to the other, and make your magic additive."

"It already is," Morgan sputtered.

"But it would be stronger still," Maeve argued.

"I am willing," I said and turned to face her.

"Well, I'm not." Morgan stamped a foot. "It pissed me off when mortals pushed women into men's arms for their own good. I'll be damned if I'll become one of those helpless damsels tethered to a man because someone was convinced I couldn't care for myself."

"You're scarcely mortal, and this will be considerably more difficult than you imagine," Maeve said dryly.

"At least consider it," Logan urged.

I sent a pointed glance winging his way. He and Maeve knew more than they'd disclosed. Logan was the last one to weigh in on the side of mate bonds.

Zeke rubbed his head against Morgan's thigh. I bet he was talking with her, hopefully counseling reason.

"I had planned to leave immediately after this meeting," Morgan said. "I will forestall my departure if you allow me a private chamber to rest and make certain of my next steps."

"You can use my rooms," I offered.

She shook her head. "Nope. Defeats the purpose. I want a place to myself where I can eat and think about how best to proceed."

"We can arrange that," Logan said.

Alarm bells clanged in my mind. Letting her out of my sight posed risks. What if she chose to leave?

I sucked in a breath. I was neither her keeper nor her jailer. In truth, I had no bond beyond simple friendship—and the fact I'd fallen in love with her. An emotion not mirrored on her end.

Sometimes, the only path is to let go. It rankled. I'm a

take-charge kind of Fae. In this instance, though, my power was nonexistent.

I bowed to her, turned, and strode from the chamber.

"Damien." Maeve's voice followed me.

"I'll be in my rooms," I called back, unable to remain in the same space with the woman I loved while she marched off to claim her destiny without me.

Would I follow her if she didn't want me to?

Holding myself back wouldn't be easy.

Trust the fates that threw us together, my inner voice suggested softly.

Since I had no choice but to comply, I set a path to my apartment determined to hang onto my pride. If Morgan wasn't called to include me in her life—Maeve's prophecies be damned—nothing I could do or say would change her mind.

CHAPTER FIVE, MORGAN

Zeke had counseled me not to be hasty. The wolf was correct, but then he usually is. We needed rest and food. Or I needed food; he'd already eaten. Logan sent one of the council members to show me to a nicely appointed room. A fire crackled cheerfully in a white-marble hearth. The wooden floor was covered with thick rugs depicting scenes of Fae glory at long-ago battles.

A good-sized bed covered with a white duvet was pushed against one wall.

"Thank you," I told him as the wolf, bird, and I made ourselves comfortable.

I hadn't caught his name, but he inclined his head. "I will have food and drink delivered presently. The fire is self-perpetuating."

Of course, it was. Before I could thank him again, he was gone.

Sita flew to a table and tucked her head under one wing.

Zeke curled up on the floor in front of the fire. Neither was about to aid in my decision-making process.

I plopped onto the bed determined to rationalize my way through an emotional storm. I cared about Damien, but we were far from a tested team. When he'd yanked me out of the boardinghouse, I'd been stunned by the scope of my magic that had actually killed several of my sister witches. Had I not been so shell shocked, I'd never have let him whisk Zeke and me out of there.

So much of this was unfamiliar territory.

I'd been almost paralyzed I'd make a mistake from the time the Coven kicked me out. That impending dread hadn't lessened. I hadn't asked anything about the Fae mating ceremony, but I felt certain it was permanent. Immortals might choose to live apart, but, if I capitulated, I'd be linked to Damien for all eternity.

Might not be such a bad thing.

I unclenched my jaw before I broke a tooth.

Maybe I should go after Hecate first. I could always revisit my future—or lack thereof—with Damien. It meant I'd be on my own, but it also meant Damien wouldn't be injured on my account.

"You'll never have all the information." Zeke wasn't asleep after all.

I stared at him, but his eyes were still closed.

He'd pointed out the crux of the matter. I had to move forward with incomplete data.

A knock on the door was followed by a tray swooping in, hovering a few moments, and then settling on a table beneath a window. A silver tankard followed, clanking onto the floor next to me. I picked it up and inhaled the sweet honey scent of aged mead.

The spiced drink slid down my throat. I swallowed again and again hoping to ease the ache in my heart. When I set the jug down, I'd emptied half of it. The tight places in my chest eased; I identified the source of my pain.

Leaving Damien was a two-edged sword. I might not be sure of my feelings for him, but walking away would be tough no matter how I tried to spin things. The look on his face when he'd left the council chamber haunted me. He was clear about what he wanted, but Faery hadn't booted him.

The Coven's abrupt dismissal had shaken my confidence more than I was willing to admit.

"Why does this have to be so hard," I muttered, pushed to my feet, and walked to the table where my dinner had materialized. I pulled out a chair but then returned for the mead before sitting. I mowed my way through fruit, cheese, warm bread, and spicy salami, washing it down with a delicate broth and more mead.

Food had a balancing effect, but it didn't point me nearer to a decision. I couldn't hide in here forever. Zeke snored softly. Sita hadn't stirred.

Time to solicit their opinions since they weren't about to offer them without prodding. I pushed the empty plate and bowl to one side, polished the remainder of the mead off, and cleared my throat before turning to Zeke and Sita.

"What do the two of you think?" I asked. Before they could answer, I draped a sloppy sound shield around us.

Damien wasn't above listening in, and I didn't want to hurt his feelings.

Zeke rolled onto his belly, head resting on outstretched paws. *"What's getting in the way?"*

"Your mother wouldn't have approved," Sita chirped, "but it's because witches never mate."

I twisted my mouth into a grimace. Yeah, out of the mouths of hawks. Were centuries of programming getting in my way? Witches were supposed to remain celibate, not that all of them did, but those who dabbled with men were damned silent about it.

And it was only for sex, never for something like a marriage.

"That's part of what's making this impossible," I told the two familiars.

"You like him," Zeke pointed out.

"Will it be enough?" I tossed back. Breath scuttled from tight lungs. "Logan said he'd prefer to see us mated. Or maybe it was Maeve, but neither said we had to be."

"Where are you heading?" Zeke cocked his head to one side.

"Nowhere is it written we can't continue as we have been," I clarified and directed my next words to Sita. "Are you planning to come when I seek out Hecate?"

The hawk spread her wings and made a couple of circuits of the chamber. "Do you want me along?"

I hesitated before answering. Sita had lost her home—and presumably her bearings—right along with me. Mother was dead. Her familiar couldn't return to the Coven, so she was a bird without a country. The Fae had offered her a forever home in Faery if she wished it, but she must feel just as out of place here as I did.

"Do you want to come with us?" I asked her. "Zeke and I would be happy to have you, but we'd understand if you chose to remain here."

The hawk landed on my shoulders and chirped, "Not sure what I want."

I nodded. "The invitation is open. You can wait until we leave to decide."

Zeke stood, padded to where I sat, and laid his muzzle on my lap. His eyes, one amber, one white, bored into my soul. *"You have my permission to add Damien to our pack."* His words were oddly formal.

Sita and I weren't the only ones treading unfamiliar ground. Zeke was the only wolf familiar I'd come across, but witches and their familiars pair bonded for eternity. I'd never given it much thought, but adding to the group would have to be a mutual decision.

I rested my hand on his head. "Thank you for making this easy."

"You still don't know what you want, though," he pointed out.

"No, and it's not going to grow clearer sitting in here."

He took the hint, moved his head, and I got to my feet. I'd told Maeve and them I needed food and rest. The food part was done, but I was unlikely to fall asleep with my mind in turmoil.

With Sita still on my shoulder and Zeke by my side, I let myself out of the room and glanced both directions. I wanted to talk with Maeve alone, but first I had to find her.

Let's be smart about this.

I opened my mind voice. *"Maeve. Are you busy?"*

"Yes, but I will make time for you."

Her response was so instantaneous, she must have been expecting me to reach out. Yeah. Of course, she was. She'd scryed it somewhere or other. Fucking seers doling out what they knew in teensy dollops. I draped a shield around my thoughts, hopefully in time. I needed her assistance, and the best way to achieve her cooperation was to erase any trace of negativity.

I started toward the council chamber before realizing I had no idea where she was and asked, *"Where are you?"*

"I will come to you."

Alrighty, then. Back inside my chamber I tidied up the remains of my meal and waited, hands clasped behind me. Zeke returned to where he'd been napping. Sita remained perched on my shoulder.

In short order, a sharp rap on the door preceded Maeve pushing it open and striding inside. Once she'd kicked it shut, power shimmered around her as she sealed us away from prying ears.

Icy blue eyes skewered me. "You could do far worse than Damien."

I avoided rolling my eyes and pointing out she wasn't mated, so why was she so hell-bent on making certain I was.

The corners of her mouth twitched.

Oh-oh. My mental ward wasn't as bulletproof as I imagined.

I spread my hands in front of me. "This isn't about me and Damien, not exactly."

"Then what is it about?" she demanded.

Truth time. I stood tall, shoulders squared. "You know more than you've said. It would help me a lot if you shared everything you know about Hecate and me."

Laughter rolled from the mage. I waited her out, annoyed she was making light of my request. Lilith, the Coven seer, had been much the same.

"I never tell anyone everything," she managed between chortles. "Why would I make an exception for you?"

"Because I'm not Fae. You don't have to ever see me again after I leave." I paused for emphasis. "I won't reveal your fall from grace, so the other Fae won't expect you to be more forthcoming in the future."

She blew out a noisy breath. "Nice try, sweetie. Your future is entangled with Damien's for as far out as I can see. Means you'll be darkening my door as well."

I closed my teeth over my lower lip, recalling what Lilith had said about her prophecies. "Just because you see something doesn't necessarily mean it will happen. Don't you gin up several alternatives, one of which comes true?"

"Aye, child. And every single future seeing I've had features you and Damien together." Moving forward, she dropped a hand onto my shoulder. "I get it. You come from a culture without men. Adding one to your life feels unnatural. Yet, here you are. There are no coincidences. You ended up in Damien's rooming house for a reason."

She shook her head. "At least I figured out why he left Faery all those years ago. It was to be positioned for when you entered his life."

"Even witches believe in free will," I protested. "And in the occasional coincidence."

"True. True. But in this instance—"

I chopped a hand downward, not caring it was rude. "Will you tell me more of what you scryed?"

There. It doesn't get more upfront and pointblank than that.

She arched white brows. "No."

"All right. I don't like it, but I respect your reasons."

"What will you do, child?"

I bit off a snappy rejoinder that I was scarcely a child, and gave her question some thought. "Two choices. I go in search of Hecate with Zeke—and perhaps Sita. Or we include Damien."

"What about the mating ceremony?"

I shook my head. "Nope. I have to be surer than I am right now before I bind myself to anyone."

She cleared her throat. "Full disclosure: the bond is permanent."

"I'd expected as much. So what happens if all of us set out absent being mated?"

"Your job will be harder, quite a bit if what I've been privy to materializes."

"I don't understand why."

Maeve set her lips in a thin line. "You're going to have to take my word for it, since you can scarcely spin the dial both ways and check which has more of a chance of success."

I ducked from beneath the hand that sat on the opposite shoulder from Sita. "Are you telling me we run the risk of failure being unmated?"

The seer nodded.

"Mmph. Still not understanding the why of it," I muttered. Maeve didn't seem in a big hurry to leave, so I kept talking. Maybe she'd slip up and reveal something useful.

"In truth, I don't understand any of this," I went on. "Presumably, Hecate created me to help corral miscreant witches who'd thrown their lot in with black magic practitioners. Yet, she vanished after trading me for Mother's baby. Not only vanished but failed to return all the years of my life. And there have been a lot of them."

I shrugged. "Makes no sense to me. If I was—"

Maeve mirrored my chopping gesture. "You cannot compare the gods with mere mages. Their timelines are not ours. Something else may have captured her attention."

"Sure. I get that, but hundreds of years have rolled past. Mother must have known things were heating up in the Coven, yet she never said a word."

"Perhaps she was spelled to silence," Maeve suggested.

"Whatever she was, it caused her demise." I shut my eyes for a moment but opened them fast when the scene from her death in the Fae infirmary flashed across the blackness.

"Her loss was tragic, but unavoidable."

I drew back as if she'd slapped me. "Nothing is unavoidable. If Zoelle had been better at reading the signs, she could have left before the Coven kidnapped her." My stomach twisted sourly; my breathing quickened. "Hell, she could have done a lot of things including telling me the truth."

"You don't know that." Maeve touched my shoulder

again. "You're getting off track. What happened to your mother was appalling, but at least she got to see you before she died. Her loss is fresh and raw for you, but it has naught to do with your current dilemma."

Before I could protest it had everything to do with it and had to be intertwined with my search for Hecate, Maeve went on, "If you do nothing, eventually, the witch goddess will seek you out."

My turn to laugh. Harsh, bitter, totally lacking in mirth. "Not very fucking likely. If she was going to seek me out, she'd have done so long since."

"You have no way of knowing, child."

"Stop calling me that." I resisted stamping a foot, which truly would have made me look like a spoiled brat.

Her eyes widened in surprise. The Fae probably never backtalked her. Crap. I truly was overstaying my welcome. Best leave before I totally alienated her.

"All right, Morgan. Is that better?"

Something about her tone grated. "Sorry," I mumbled.

She backed up until she leaned against a wall watching me rather like a cat might eye a mouse. "This isn't any easier for us than it is for you," she said. "There are salient reasons differing types of mages rarely join forces unless a major battle is afoot. We view the world through different eyes. I was trying to make you feel more comfortable. Instead, you took it as an affront."

"It's scarcely an excuse, but I used to be more trusting."

Zeke pressed against my thigh, offering moral support. Sita's talons dug a bit deeper.

"Hang onto every scrap of skepticism." Maeve angled

her head to one side. "The Coven structure protected you from the world. You lack life experience beyond its boundaries. It's another argument for you not going by yourself. Damien told me about the carnage at the boardinghouse. For whatever reason, your power has expanded. I've sensed changes over the brief time I've known you."

My head pounded. This conversation had slipped well beyond my control, and I was deep into feeling overwhelmed. "Your point?"

"Someone needs to be a sounding board for your increased ability. Heading into the world by yourself in search of deities no one's seen for centuries is bound to land you in situations where you loose that power. If it comes to anyone's attention, you'll end up in the same mess Damien did: captured by the PDA."

"Give me credit for a few smarts," I sputtered.

She looked askance at me. "Are you intimating Damien was nabbed because he's stupid?"

Heat flowed from my neck upward until I had to be beet red. Damn it. She was a master at putting me on the defensive.

"You need him," she continued. "He could do the wise thing and remain in Faery, but standing by your side means more to him than his own safety."

Of course, she'd support her kinsman. Too bad that support painted me into a corner as an ungrateful witch.

"If you're trying to change my mind, it's not working," I gritted.

"I wasn't aware you'd come to a decision that needed

changing." She arched a white brow.

I hadn't, but it was beside the point. "I don't have the energy to spar with you," I said. "I'm tired and grieving and confused. My life turned on its axis, and I'm finding my way, but it's not easy."

"When I'm not sure what to do, I wait until the path forward becomes clearer."

"Not sure I have that luxury." I hesitated. "You said Hecate would come to me, but I don't believe it."

Maeve shrugged and pushed away from the wall. "This conversation is about over."

What a joke. It had been over from the moment she walked into my borrowed chamber. Any lingering illusions I'd had about the Fae accepting me as one of them went up in smoke. They'd been kind because of Damien.

Maeve headed for the door.

I followed with the animals in tow, pushing through before she could shut it. "I know what I'm doing," I announced.

Maeve turned back toward me. "Feel like sharing?"

"I will tell everyone at the same time. Does the council chamber work? Or is there a better, less formal, location?"

The air around her glistened as she raised her mind voice. I caught echoes in Gaelic, but far from everything. Nodding briskly, she said, "Follow me."

"What are we doing?" Zeke asked.

Sita clacked her beak a time or two.

I didn't answer. If I told him, Maeve would intercept our mindspeech. As I trailed after her robed form, I finetuned what I wanted to say to whomever showed up.

CHAPTER SIX, DAMIEN

Hiding in my rooms like a jilted lover didn't sit well. After a short time, I made my way to the library to educate myself about Hecate. Sitting in the midst of ancient vellum books and scrolls, it was clear I'd made up my mind. Even if Morgan wanted to go it alone, I'd track her, remaining on the sidelines until she needed me.

I couldn't imagine a task of this magnitude where my skills wouldn't come in handy. Once I popped out of nowhere and provided timely assistance, her antipathy about having me along would dissipate.

Or I hoped it would.

Greek goddess and daughter to Perseus and Astaria, Hecate had played far more roles than I anticipated. Goddess of sacred animals, portals, liminal spaces, and the moon, she'd had a rich and varied life before Circe and Medea joined forces with her. After that, she was solidly in the witch camp. They worshipped her, and she repaid their loyalty in kind.

What in the hell had happened to the two of them? They'd dropped out of sight too.

Try as I might, I couldn't find anything about renegade witches or the goddess intervening to save her minions. Perhaps the information was too new to be memorialized in writing. Our library was self-replenishing. Unlike human libraries, new material showed up frequently all on its own.

Still, Morgan was hundreds of years old. Granted the goddess might have a different take on time than the rest of us immortals, but it was bothersome she hadn't resurfaced in all the years since Morgan's making. I suspected she'd thought better of the original idea behind Morgan's existence.

If I was correct, she might be furious to be confronted with evidence of a failed plan. Best case, she'd tell Morgan and Zeke to get lost. Worst case, she'd turn her ire on them, however it shaped up.

Another element that didn't sit right was Zoelle's long silence. Clearly, Morgan's mother had known a lot. She might have been sworn to silence, or perhaps Hecate had selectively eradicated parts of her memory. The latter seemed unlikely, though.

I had considerably more questions than answers. So what else was new?

I was just reaching for another volume when Maeve's mind voice suggested I make haste to one of our smaller dining rooms. Apparently, Morgan had picked a direction.

Bolting upright, I started out of the library but got hold

of myself. Turning, I instructed my source materials to return to their places on the shelves. No reason to leave the room a mess.

Since I'd already made my decision, I toyed with telling Maeve I'd sit this one out, but it would make me look weak. I'd thrown down a gauntlet when I said I was agreeable with the mating ceremony. Only a coward was so intimidated by the specter of unwelcome news they failed to suit up and show up.

Regardless, running from failure wasn't me. I'd see this through. I'd already picked my own path, even if she said she was going in search of the witch goddess without me. Once the last scroll tucked itself neatly into place, I set a course for the indicated dining room. I walked with a measured pace, neither unduly fast nor dragging my feet. While en route, I wrapped shielding around my mind and worked on a neutral expression.

Why was I so certain we were destined to be together? Was it wishful thinking on my part?

I lacked objective evidence beyond my intuition, but it had never failed me before. The journey lasted forever and was over in the space between two breaths. When I walked beneath the lintel, Morgan, Zeke, Sita, Maeve, and Logan were already there.

"Thought you weren't coming," Maeve muttered.

Surprise ran through me. Had it taken longer than I thought to traverse the short distance?

"Sorry. I was in the library, and I took a moment to return my source materials to their proper spots. I hate finding the place a mess."

"You're damn near the only one who uses it," Logan noted.

"Scarcely my fault," I retorted.

"No one said it was," he murmured. Waves of a calming spell wafted my way. I sidestepped them.

Zeke trotted to me and licked my hand. I scratched between his furry ears and transferred my attention to Morgan. Unlike Zeke, she wasn't looking at me, which didn't bode well. Last thing I wanted was to make her uncomfortable.

Spots of color rode high on her pale skin, tinting her cheekbones a rose shade. Beyond the display of heightened emotion, she stood tall, shoulders rolled back. Sita made a cooing noise, not unlike a mourning dove.

Great. My inner turmoil was so obvious, the animals were comforting me. Zeke moved from my hand to pressing his head against my thigh.

"This is hard," Morgan blurted. The color in her face deepened. "When I walked in here, I had a plan mapped out, but suddenly it's less clear."

The promise I'd made to myself to remain silent and hear her out vanished. I couldn't stand to see her looking so distressed. "For what it's worth"—I looked straight at her and hoped she'd scrape her gaze up off the floor—"my research topic du jour was Hecate. I know a lot more about her now, but nothing I came across shed light on your dilemma."

"Why would you do that?" Morgan's gaze finally, finally met mine.

"Because I care about what happens to you, and I was

hoping to find something that might shorten your search, make it simpler." I paused to take a breath. "I did locate what was once her primary home. It's a cave on one of the Greek islands. At least it's a place to begin."

"You're going to follow me regardless, huh?" Her mismatched eyes pinched at their corners.

Truth time. I nodded slowly. Saying no, and then popping up later, didn't mesh well with being candid.

"But the only reason I want to do this alone is to protect you," she said.

"For the love of Danu," Maeve sputtered. "This thing is so much bigger than either of you. Get over yourselves."

Zeke woofed, chiding the seer for criticizing his mistress. Sita clacked her beak.

Logan chuckled and nudged Maeve. "You foresaw this."

I swiveled my head in her direction along with a pointed glance. "You always know more than you reveal, but if there are things that could help us—er, Morgan, if she goes alone —now is the time to divulge them."

"Same thing I said to her." Morgan set her lips in a tight line.

Logan nudged Maeve again.

The seer arched white brows and twisted her features into a grimace. A sphere maybe eighteen inches in diameter materialized out of nowhere, suspended before her.

Maeve didn't bother with words. The globe took on an inner glow. Scenes formed, tumbling atop each other. I stared intently, committing them to memory. In the first, Maeve and Zeke were alone on a barren plain. Triple suns beat down as they trudged across what looked like an off-world version of the Sahara. A dragonesque figure, blood-red with leathery wings, filled the sky before that vision ended.

The second scene also had them alone, but this time in a thickly wooded glen, trudging through creeks, brush, and mud. A gnarled oak cracked open, and a dryad stepped out.

Unlike the few I've run across, this one looked evil with pointed teeth, hands curled into claws, and the stench of poison dripping from her open mouth.

"Where are these places?" Morgan asked.

Logan shook his head. "Quiet. If you talk, the images will stop."

As if to underscore the truth in his words, the globe dimmed so much I couldn't make out the next scene for a while. When it shaped up, I'd joined the group, and we were somewhere dark. Probably underground judging from the feel of the place.

With little warning, creatures ran at us, their red eyes glowing in the dark. About the size of large beavers with matted black fur and gleaming teeth, they herded us toward something. No dialogue in the vision, but we cycled through magics in a futile attempt to break free. Zeke killed one after another until his snout was streaked crimson.

No matter how many he killed, more rose from somewhere.

A dozen more images followed. I was in some, but far from all. Each featured a challenging landscape and some type of animal that wanted us dead. I filed the information away and kept on watching.

No wonder Maeve held silence most of the time.

Interpreting these diverse bits and pieces of data into some sort of whole that made sense was beyond me. I started to tell her I'd seen enough when something new entered the latest environment: a high mountain vista marked by snowcapped peaks and ice-coated rocks.

This time, rather than magical beasts, a caped and hooded figure marched toward us. Tall, angular, bony fingers circled by gold and silver rings, she tossed the cowl covering her head back revealing a high forehead, piercing dark eyes, and long dark hair streaked with silver.

She extended an arm, pointing directly at me. "Go back to Faery," she rasped. "You are not needed here."

Morgan and Zeke stepped between me and the goddess before the scene blacked out.

"What does all that mean?" I demanded. "Other than the goddess has to be Hecate."

Maeve shrugged. "Could mean a whole lot of things. *This* is why I choose to hold information close. If you and Morgan are mated, 'twill make it harder for Hecate to jettison you. Beyond the witch goddess, you will face many problems. Your magic will be more...cooperative if your lives are joined."

"I'm more confused than I was to start with," Morgan mumbled.

"I wasn't there at all," Sita cawed, feathers drooping.

"Doesn't mean you can't go if you want," Maeve told the hawk.

"Maybe it means I'd be inconsequential," she squawked.

I beckoned to her, but the bird remained perched on Morgan's shoulder. She'd had a rough go losing everything dear to her just as Morgan had. Except Morgan had Zeke. Sita had no one—except us.

Morgan stroked her feathers. "I would always welcome you."

Sita spread her wings and flew circles around the room.

"I walked into this meeting determined to go alone." Morgan spoke slowly. "Despite Maeve's visions, it seems the wisest path. The Coven may have kicked me out, but I'm still a witch. My people are in trouble. Helping where I can must be my first priority."

She walked close enough to lay a hand on my arm. "Please don't take this wrong. It's not that I don't care about you. I do, but I have to put my sisters first. Not all of them have fallen into darkness."

Teeth closed over her lower lip hard enough spots of blood bloomed. "If anything happened to you, I'd never forgive myself. Beyond that, inter-mage pairings are so rare I've never heard of one. Makes me wonder how well ours would fare. It's not something I want to find out once we've bound ourselves with blood and magic for eternity."

"What if I feel the same way?" I countered.

"What do you mean? Same way about what?"

"If anything happened to you, and I wasn't there, I'd spend all my days mourning and kicking myself for not insisting on accompanying you."

"No way to satisfy everyone." Morgan sounded sad.

Zeke licked my hand again. Sita was still flying circles around us.

Maeve's globe came alive once more. This time, it was awash in red. Armies marched, mages fell and rose to fight again. Trolls, dwarfs, demons, Fae, witches, and others I couldn't identify battled one another.

My heart ached; sadness rolled through me. Was I witnessing the death of magic?

"What is this?" Logan mirrored the despondence I felt.

"One of many possibilities." Maeve's usually melodic voice was strained. "I have no idea if it's related to the Coven's fall from grace, but if I don't figure this out, our kind may well be doomed along with every other white mage."

"Are all your visions so difficult to interpret?" I asked.

A corner of her mouth turned downward. "Nay. Only the most critical ones."

A whole new respect for her dawned. I'd had no idea the weight she carried with her indecipherable psychic sendings. "Have you asked Zoe and Bess what they think?"

She nodded. "Of course. There's strength in numbers, and we've been seers to the Fae since the Celts made us."

"We should go together." Zeke woofed. *"Sita too."*

Morgan held up a hand. "I'm going to propose a compromise. I will leave on my own and take a shot at finding Hecate. Once I've either found her—or given up—I'll return and join forces with the rest of you."

"What if Hecate forbids it?" Maeve asked.

Morgan shrugged. "I'm my own witch. No one dictates to me."

The seer tilted her head to one side. "Big words. They may fall before the one who made you, particularly since she probably programmed a minimal level of compliance. No one creates minions without it."

"Guess I'll find out."

"You're making a mistake," Zeke said in mind speech all of us could hear.

"Perhaps, but it will be my mistake and won't put Damien or any of the other Fae in danger on our account," she replied.

The wolf whined. He didn't like her response, but he'd follow her no matter where she went.

Sita returned to Morgan's shoulder. "I choose to accompany you and Zeke."

The globe had vanished. Maeve reached into a pocket and withdrew two crystals, perhaps a few inches long. She handed one to Morgan and the other to me.

"Following her is not wise. It's one option I haven't scryed. These crystals will allow primitive communication over distance. Morgan, if you run into difficulties, don't be a hero; grasp the crystal and think of Damien. His crystal will light, and he'll do his damnedest to locate you."

Morgan hesitated before transferring her crystal to a pocket. I held mine, feeling it warm my palm.

"Do you want to take anything for your journey?" I asked Morgan.

She shook her head. "I left garments in the council chamber. If you could set them aside for me, I'd appreciate it. We'll figure things out as we go. I have a feeling that time grows short, but I have no idea where it's coming from. The sooner we're on our way, the better."

"How will you get to Greece?" I was full of questions to mask a sense of foreboding marching down my spine.

"Obviously, I won't. Witches can't teleport across oceans, so it's not where I'll begin."

"What is?" Maeve asked.

"I'm not sure. Perhaps one of the other Covens. Maybe the Mer people. I can't answer until I'm out there looking."

"Take this." Logan thrust a small leather bag at her.

Morgan didn't make any move to grab the sack. "What's in it?"

"Money. Food. Credit cards and passable identification. You won't get far without them."

My eyes widened. I'd had no idea my kin had access to forged documents. I'd wasted ungodly amounts of money on the dark web having them crafted to support my stay among mortals.

"Thank you." Morgan reached for the bag. "Thank you very much. It's more than I deserve after all the trouble I've caused you."

"You did not cause this trouble, child," Maeve reassured her. "While your presence was s lynchpin, events surrounding you were scripted long before your Coven kicked fate into gear by banishing you."

"If you say so," Morgan murmured. "Best not to prolong this. We're ready to leave."

Zeke's ears and tail drooped. He licked my hand one last time. I ran my fingers through his rough outer coat. "This isn't goodbye," I reminded him.

He tilted his head, and a mournful howl filled the dining room. It chilled me even more than the visions in Maeve's crystal ball.

"May I walk you out?" I asked.

"Better if you don't," she said and turned to leave.

Logan sprinted after her, Zeke, and Sita. "I will see you safely to our border."

Morgan kept on walking.

Once they were gone, Maeve turned to me. "How are you doing?"

I shrugged. "Hard to say." My hand still gripped the crystal hard enough its edges cut into my hand.

"Come with me." She beckoned.

"Where are we going?"

"You were onto something researching Hecate. We're going to dig deeper and see what we can find."

Because I didn't have anything better to do, I trailed after her. Maeve's research might yield more than mine, but I was onto her. The more time that elapsed between Morgan's leave-taking and me possibly tracking her, the lower the odds of finding her easily.

"I know what you're up to," I muttered.

Maeve stopped dead and turned toward me. "The hell you do. Pull your head out of your ass and act like the Fae you are. What's afoot is far larger than you and the witch."

Shame swamped me. I avoided mumbling, *yes, Mother,* and hightailed it after her as she sprinted down one of Faery's many corridors. Morgan's magic outpaced mine by a factor of ten—maybe twenty. It pained me to admit it, but she was more than capable of taking care of herself.

CHAPTER SEVEN, MORGAN

I figured Logan had something he wanted to impart privately, but I was wrong. When we got to the veils separating Faery from Earth, he said, "You've been to this spot often enough to find it easily. If you return, call my name three times. I will hear and let you inside."

I tossed the strap of the leather sack over one shoulder. "Thank you for everything. You've been more than kind."

"The world is a harsh and unforgiving mistress. Wishing you success, although I fear you will not find that which you seek. Not without unrelenting pain and sacrifice."

On that cheery note, he vanished, leaving Zeke, Sita, and me beyond Faery's gates. I didn't remember traversing them, yet we had.

"What he said didn't make sense," Zeke noted.

"Huh? In what way?"

"He said you wouldn't find Hecate," Sita replied.

"*But then he said pain and sacrifice were the cost,*" Zeke chimed in.

I pinched the bridge of my nose between my thumb and forefinger. Where to begin? I should have asked Damien what he'd discovered in the Fae library.

Should have.

Yeah, should've done a whole bunch of stuff. Why had I been so all-fired determined to do this by myself?

To keep Damien safe, an inner voice reminded me.

Also, this wasn't his battle. Neither was it a Fae problem. I'd created inter-species problems when I'd dragged Fae along to rescue Mother from a dungeon in the Old Country. The Fae had barely seen the beginnings of the fallout from that, let alone the end.

Feeling marginally better—and desperately alone—I mapped out what to do first. The Mer people had been kind to me when I'd been hunting for Damien after the paranormal police shanghaied him. Often they knew things other mages didn't because of their link with the sea. It spanned the globe, and water carried information like no other medium.

"*If we go there again,*" Zeke announced, "*leave me on shore.*"

The hawk cawed agreement.

Meant we'd need a spot far more private than Seattle's waterfront, the place we'd launched from last time. I visualized one of hundreds of small islands in the San Juan chain and set a journey spell in motion.

The space between summoning the casting and arrival was breath stealingly short. My power was like a live thing, champing at the bit for expression. Maybe I could make it all the way across the Atlantic, but I didn't want to test it unless I had to.

If I did, I should test it alone. Zeke and Sita would object, but I couldn't subject them to that big an unknown.

An image of Damien flickered behind my lids. I shut it down. I'd made my choice. Best not grow too dependent on him—or anyone else. Ever since the Coven kicked me out, I'd essentially been on my own. He'd made me forget that, and it wasn't wise.

"He helped you with a whole lot," Zeke observed.

"And he saved my life," Sita reminded me.

Great. My animal sidekicks thought I'd made a shit decision to leave Damien behind. Nothing I could do about it now.

"You could go back," the wolf said.

Having him constantly sifting through my thoughts wasn't helpful.

"We're here now." I spread my arms wide to encompass an empty windswept beach surrounded by cliffs. On the northern edge of the San Juans on a small island without a name.

"Find a comfortable spot to wait for me. At least it's not raining."

"There are caves in the cliffs if it does," Sita squawked.

"Maybe I should go with you." Zeke nudged me.

I knelt in front of him and stroked his fur. "I'll be fine. Back in an hour or so."

"Don't forget the crystal," Zeke woofed.

Ambivalence ruled. Hanging onto the crystal defeated

my goal of being independent, but what if being stiff necked meant I couldn't get back to Zeke and Sita because something unexpected popped up?

I'd dropped the stone into the sack with the money and food. After retrieving it, I stashed the bag under several rocks and committed the location to memory. The shoreline was littered with rocks, and they all looked alike.

As ready as I was likely to be, I walked to the shoreline, opened my mind voice, and sang the Mer people's song. A mermaid popped from the surf. Violet hair shrouded her. Matching violet eyes took me in.

"What is it now?" she asked. "Is your Fae missing again?"

I started to inquire how she knew about my last sojourn with her people, but didn't. Probably my quest to rescue Damien had become common knowledge.

"I am here on my own. I seek knowledge of Hecate."

"What kind of knowledge?"

I turned my hands palms upward. "Anything. Where she is. What she's been doing these past several centuries."

The mermaid's head bobbed. She had a pointed chin, angular cheekbones, and rings on several fingers. "Figures you would want to know. You're her creation. I sense her blood in your veins."

Even the Fae hadn't said that. Their healers had determined I wasn't directly related to Mother, but their assessment stopped there.

We stood staring at one another as waves crashed against the shore. The wind was picking up; leaden clouds threatened rain.

"Will you help me?"

"Not sure. I've passed your request up the line."

I hadn't sensed her using telepathy, but it didn't matter. Shifting from foot to foot, I waited. The wind cut through my garments, so I directed a thin flow of magic to keep my feet and fingers from freezing.

Zeke and Sita joined me on the shoreline.

"A witch with two familiars," the mermaid murmured. "I read about this in the lore, but it was long ago."

"Do you recall what it said?"

She shook her head before glancing upward. "Come with me. Our regent will grant you a brief audience."

Brief sounded promising. The Mer people are nothing if not raconteurs.

"Back soon," I told the animals and followed the mermaid into the waves. Once the water grew deep enough to cover my head, I switched to extracting oxygen from it. It's a simple enough skill. Probably should have left my garments on the shore. Drying them would take time, and wearing them soaking wet would be uncomfortable.

Should have learned from my last go round.

The sea's bottom dropped abruptly, reminding me of the difference between the mainland and islands. I swam through murky water, keeping the mermaid's tail in sight. After a while, we came to a structure not unlike the one I'd visited recently.

Constructed of rocks and coral, it glowed softly from swathes of iridescent lichen. We swam through an open window and into a richly appointed chamber decorated with shells, glittering stones, and gold and silver ornaments. Had they come from a shipwreck?

A striking male swam my way. Dark hair long enough to reach his waist swirled around him. Turquoise eyes carried a sharp intelligence. His tail was blue-and-green scales.

"I am Reginald, one of several regents to the Mer people." He held out a hand. When I clasped it, a shot of power blasted through me.

I tried to yank my hand away but got nowhere.

"A good lesson for you, witch," he said. "Never touch another mage unless you are certain of their intentions." He released my fingers.

The mermaid who'd led me here treaded water off to one side.

"Marquessa tells me you come seeking knowledge of Hecate," he went on.

Hmmm. Marquessa had to be my guide.

"I do. Any information is welcome since I know nothing."

"Not totally true. You are aware she created you."

I nodded. *"I have only recently come by that bit of knowledge. Beyond that, nothing."*

"Hecate has been missing for hundreds of years. It struck some as odd. At one point, Circe and Medea launched an inquiry. Turned out a few of the other Greek gods didn't care for her plan to elevate you over witchdom, so they made certain she wouldn't be able to see her plan through to its conclusion.

"At that point Circe and Medea made themselves scarce. No one's seen them, either, for many a long year.

"Do you mean they're all dead?" My mind voice had a hitch. With Mother dead, and now Hecate…

"Don't be ridiculous. They're immortal."

"So was Mother, but the Coven killed her."

Dark brows shot up. "I did not know that."

"What did the other gods do to Hecate?" I pressed.

"Barricaded her in her cave. From what I can glean, she's still there."

Ha. Explained why she'd never reached out to me. *"Um, where precisely is it?"*

"But she's your goddess, and you do not know?"

Irritation scratched a path through me. *"If I did, I wouldn't have asked."*

"Beneath the ruins of Lagina where a temple in her honor used to stand."

"Is it in Greece?"

"Nay, in southwest Turkey, in an area named Caria. Borders have changed with the years."

I inclined my head. *"Thank you. I won't take up any more of your time."* He'd said our meeting would be brief, and I had to figure out how to cross the Atlantic.

"What's your hurry, little witch? Stay. Share a meal with me."

Something about the way he was looking at me made me uncomfortable. If I read him correctly, he was expecting favors in exchange for information.

"I appreciate the offer, truly I do, but I cannot eat while under water. Perhaps another time." I bowed. *"My familiars are waiting for me, and I have many miles to cover."*

"Hecate isn't going anywhere."

No, but I am.

After bowing again, I turned and swam through the same window I'd entered, setting a course for shore. I half expected him—or someone—to come after me, but no one did.

Had I made a mistake? Had my refusal to share food alienated him? No way of knowing. Besides, if I'd been correct and he was angling for intimacy, things would have become awkward quickly. I might be ambivalent about Damien, but I wasn't about to invite anyone else into my bed.

The sea bottom rose up to meet me. Getting my feet under me, I trudged out of the surf, wet garments clinging to my body. A stiff wind blew; I shivered. Zeke ran to me. Sita landed on my shoulder. Both of them peppered me with questions.

I set a course for an opening in rocks lining the beach, intent on drying my clothing. Along the way, I detoured long enough to pick up the sack Logan had sent along.

"Give me a minute," I told them and ducked into a smallish cavern. Its sandy bottom was wet, but at least rock walls cut the wind.

Starting with my boots and socks, I stripped down to bare skin and spread my top, jacket, and pants on flat rocks after I'd wrung water out of them. A judicious shot of magic would hurry them along. They didn't have to be totally dry, but anything was better than their current condition.

I was sparing with additional power to keep myself on the upside of freezing. I'd need every iota at my disposal to cross the ocean.

"Well?" Sita cawed from a rock where she'd perched when I started disrobing.

"The reason Hecate never sought me out was because some of her fellow gods didn't like her plans for me. So, they imprisoned her in a cave."

"Is she still there?" Zeke asked.

I shrugged. "Not sure."

"Where is it?" Sita chirped.

"Across the Atlantic Ocean in a country called Turkey."

Zeke woofed once; his tail plumed. *"See. I knew we'd need Damien."* He added magic to mine to hurry my clothing along.

I crossed my arms beneath my breasts to conserve what little body heat I had. "Not sure about that. My power has expanded. I may be able to get there on my own."

"What happens if you fail?" Zeke stared at me with his mismatched eyes.

The wolf is good at asking hard questions.

"I could get stuck in the in-between spot."

"Define stuck," Sita chirped.

"If I run through all my magic, I'll have to wait until it replenishes itself." I blew out a tight breath. These were my companions; lying to them didn't sit well. "The problem with that," I went on, "is the space we use to teleport doesn't tolerate mages hanging about. It could trap me indefinitely, cut off my air, or do a number of unpleasant things."

"Damien will help," Zeke woofed.

"I need to think this through better," I told him and Sita. Fingering my top, I figured it was dry enough and slipped it over my head. My pants and jacket took a few minutes longer. What moisture was left would dry on my body. Last, I donned socks and tied my boots into place.

I culled through the sack from Logan. It contained four thousand dollars. My eyes widened at the amount. I could rent a hotel room, eat something, and map out how to proceed. Had I known there was that much money in the bag, I'd have been more careful with it. I pulled out a pastry filled with cheese and divided it among us.

Organizing the bills, I tucked them into an inner pocket of my jacket along with a driver's license, an American Express card, and a Visa. I guessed I could pay with credit cards and save the cash. If I didn't spend it, I'd return it to Logan.

I stepped outside the cave. The weather had done nothing but go downhill. Rain pelted from leaden skies, and the wind was a live thing, shrieking imprecations as it tried to rip my hair out at the roots.

"Back inside," I said.

"*Where are we going?*" Zeke asked.

I built a hasty map of the San Juans in my mind. "Anacortes. We'll find a hotel and spend tonight there. How do you feel about a glamour that makes you smaller?"

He scrunched his face and woofed.

I crouched in front of him. "A lot of motels take dogs, but not so many take big ones."

"*Just don't make me a poodle.*"

I laughed. "Deal."

"What about me?" Sita squawked.

"I'll open the window once we're inside."

Because I'd never been to Anacortes, and it was still daylight, I aimed for a spot half a mile outside the city. Lady Luck was with us. I didn't surprise so much as a coyote when we emerged in thick timber. I worked on Zeke's glamour until he looked like an Australian Shepherd, a small one.

Satisfied his disguise would pass muster, I hurried into town. Sita paced us from the air.

I took my time and located the seedier part of town. A Motel 6 had a marquee that said it was pet friendly, so I started there. Before I went in, I fashioned a leash from magic and tethered Zeke to me.

No one was behind the glassed-in front desk, so I rang the bell. Minutes ticked past until a slender fiftyish East Indian male wearing a wrinkled white shirt and black pants walked through a door at the back of the reception area. The odor of tobacco clung to him.

He looked me up and down; I was dripping on his floor.

"Help you?" he inquired in a tone suggesting he was an inch from telling me to get my soaking-wet ass out of there.

"I'd like a room for the night, please." I added a smidge of compulsion to my request.

"The dog is extra."

Zeke woofed. It came out high pitched to match his current glamour.

I reached into my coat pocket and drew out my fake driver's license and the American Express card. Good thing I'd glanced at them. My new name was Clara Hilton.

"It's okay about my dog," I told him and passed both items beneath the glass.

"Ain't you even going to ask how much?" Suspicion lined his words.

"Um, I saw an ad. Isn't it something like forty bucks?"

He snickered. "Nice try, lady. Nope. It's sixty-five. The dog is an extra twenty."

"That's fine." I deepened the compulsion. I wanted to get out of this lobby and into a hot shower.

He picked up the driver's license, held it up, and stared at me before setting it down and fingering the AmEx card. "You got anything else, miss?"

"Why?"

"Boss don't like it when we take this one."

I considered asking why not. Instead, I handed over a Visa card.

He hunched in front of a computer, punched a bunch of keys, and gave me something to sign. I had the M in Morgan completed before I changed it to a C and signed the name that matched my ID.

Crap. A lot to remember here.

He passed my ID and both credit cards back. I tucked them away.

"Here you go. Room 114. It's to the left and halfway down. Checkout is eleven sharp. Coffee in the lobby starting at six a.m."

"Thanks." I took the room key card and Zeke and I walked out of the office.

"Seemed strange," Zeke muttered.

"He didn't think we had the money to stay here," I explained in a soft voice. "Probably has to ask a lot of people to leave."

Room 114 was on our right. I slid the card into the slot and pushed the door open. Zeke trotted in after me, shucking his glamour the moment the door shut. Both the door and the window faced the street. Since it was simpler, I stepped back outside, raised my mind voice, and called Sita.

Once she flew toward me, I cloaked her in invisibility and ushered her inside.

She shook water from her feathers. I undressed for the second time in the last hour, but, this time, I hung my clothes from hooks and hangers and disappeared into the bathroom intent on a scalding shower. There was soap, but no shampoo.

When I emerged, much warmer and cleaner, the wolf and hawk were asleep. Zeke had curled up on the bed, and Sita perched on a dresser under the TV.

Rather than wasting magic drying my things, I pushed Zeke over and crawled into bed, pulling the ratty blanket and bedspread up to my chin. They were filthy, but the sheets smelled of bleach.

I silently blessed the Fae who'd thought to provision me.

The sleep that had eluded me in Faery hovered, wanting to claim me for a few blessed hours. I fought it before giving in. What I really needed was to figure out how I'd travel to Turkey, but my mind pedaled in weary circles.

And how I'd break it to Zeke and Sita that they couldn't come. Not on this first transoceanic jaunt.

Every solution came with insoluble problems.

I've always been better when I'm fresh, so I shut my eyes. I'd rest, grab a meal from a diner I'd seen across the street, and take things from there.

CHAPTER EIGHT, DAMIEN

The Fae library had hidden rooms I didn't know about. Maeve led me through a revolving bookshelf and into a secondary library.

"What's this?" I asked once I picked my jaw up off the floor. How could this place exist? Books and scrolls I'd never seen beckoned like an arcane candy shop.

"What does it look like?" she countered.

I shook my head. "Poor phrasing. What I should have asked is why I didn't know about this before."

"Because it's mine. I'm trusting you to hold silence."

Alright, then.

I wanted to ask where she'd procured everything. I didn't. She wouldn't have told me, anyway. Thousands more scrolls and eldritch volumes lined every wall of two medium-sized rooms.

A selection plopped onto tables.

"Start there." She pointed. "Not another word till you've found something useful."

Maeve's always been temperamental, but I'd never seen this side of her before. Condescending and abrupt, she clearly hated sharing her secret stash—with anyone. I sat in the indicated spot, pulled a scroll in front of me, and began reading.

She settled at a different table.

Hours passed. I located paper and a pen and jotted notes from some of the more promising source documents. Deep into the fifth scroll, I stifled a gasp.

"What?" Maeve's tone was sharp. Maybe she didn't enjoy research.

I shot to my feet and carried the scroll to where she sat. "Look at this." I tapped the aged vellum gently.

She scanned, unrolling as she went, and slapped a hand on the table. "That's it, then. Why Hecate never claimed Morgan."

"Certainly seems likely," I agreed. "She was imprisoned to stymie her plan."

Breath rattled from Maeve. "This poses a whole new set of problems."

"Like what? We'll figure out where she is and free her." I dusted my hands together.

Ice-blue eyes bored into me. "You're not thinking. The same gods—or goddesses—who were upset enough about this plan to shanghai one of their own won't welcome Morgan with open arms. Or us."

"They won't welcome her at all," I mumbled, feeling naïve for not appreciating that immediately.

"Indeed. Quite the opposite. If you interfere, retribution will be swift. Vengeance might extend to us all."

"Crap. We have to warn her," I said, worry cutting deep.

"Agreed, but look at this bit I was reading." She pushed a book with crumbling pages to the far side of the table.

I scanned from the top of the page and turned to the next until I finished the section. "Who wrote this one?" I asked while looking at the frontispiece. It didn't tell me much. Some fellow named Bjorn Prather had penned a series of prophecies in the 1400s.

"He's a Celtic seer," Maeve explained. "Morgan is now a witch with two familiars, so I believe this prediction refers to her."

"Surely, she can't be the only one," I protested. "This divination suggests a witch with two familiars will fail in her task and end up cursed, forfeiting everything dear to her."

A sudden chill tracked down my spine.

Maeve pushed to her feet. "I had decided to leave her be—and we may still do that. Still, she deserves the luxury of information."

"I still think we should free Hecate."

"She's already free."

I looked askance at the seer. "And you know this how?"

"How do you think? Come on." She crooked a finger and started for the revolving bookcase.

"Don't you want to put things away."

"Later. Far more critical tasks lie ahead."

The main library was deserted as usual. No wonder no one suspected Maeve's personal collection existed.

"Change into something fresh," she told me. "Bring warm clothes. I'll meet you at the veils in a quarter hour."

I'm not normally especially biddable, but I followed her instructions. She had something in mind. More importantly, she had Morgan's best interests at heart. It was a point of agreement.

We walked out of Faery into the dark velvet of night on Earth. From the looks of things, it was around eight in the evening, perhaps nine.

"Where is she?" Maeve asked.

I hadn't looked, but I did now, courtesy of my crystal, and zeroed in on the small town of Anacortes on Fidalgo Island. We'd have to be closer for better accuracy. I sent a series of images to Maeve, and asked, "Your spell or mine?"

She shrugged. For the barest of moments weariness settled over her ageless features like a shadow. The seer has always known more than she's cared to reveal. I'd only recently appreciated how heavy a burden her knowledge was.

Pulling from the earth beneath my feet, I fashioned a journey casting, draped it over us both, and kindled it. I wasn't especially careful regarding our destination, so I added invisibility to the mix.

We came out on a mostly deserted residential street. Under cover of a grove of trees, I loosed both parts of my spell and set a tracking one in motion. Morgan was about two miles away.

"She's maybe a twenty-minute walk," I told Maeve.

The seer had changed from her customary robe into modern garb. Trousers, boots, and a jacket, all in black. Rain sluiced down on us. She fashioned shielding and motioned for me to lead out.

The scenery changed from houses to a seedy business district. My tracker pointed straight at the Motel 6. I silently applauded Morgan for a solid choice in a nondescript part of town.

So we wouldn't surprise her, I raised my mind voice. *"Morgan, we're close."*

"What? Why? Who is we? And how close?"

"Maeve is with me. We unearthed vital information."

Morgan didn't reply, so I closed the distance to room 114 and knocked on the door. I could have opened it with magic, but it would have been disrespectful. Bad enough we'd chased her down after she told us she wanted to go it alone.

Morgan tugged the door open and motioned us inside, her face an unreadable mask. She'd wrapped a bedspread around herself, probably because her clothes were drying. She'd been out in the same downpour as us.

Zeke jumped on me, paws on my shoulders as he licked my face effusively. Sita squawked and flew rings around the spartan room. At least the animals were happy to see me.

I squelched that oh-poor-me line of thought and glanced at Morgan. Dark hair spilled down her shoulders. Circles etched beneath her eyes. Gathering her in my arms to comfort her wouldn't have been met with appreciation, so I said, "Apologies for tracking you."

Dark brows crawled up her forehead like crow's wings.

"Did you want to dress?" Maeve inquired.

"No point. My garments are still wet. They never did dry

out from my visit with the Mer people, and since then it's done nothing but rain."

Sita settled on my shoulder. Zeke's paws were on the floor, but he clung to my side as if he were my familiar, not Morgan's.

She leaned against a wall and pulled the spread tighter around her tall, spare figure. Full breasts pushed against the fabric. I averted my gaze.

"We discovered why Hecate never claimed you," Maeve began.

Morgan nodded tiredly. "Yeah. Already found that out from the Mer people. Apparently, she's imprisoned beneath some shrine in Turkey. I was figuring out how to get there."

"Are you sure you want to?" Maeve cocked her head to one side.

"Why wouldn't I?"

The seer blew out a tense breath. "Think about it, child. Those who imprisoned her won't take kindly to intervention. Do you really want to position yourself squarely on their shit list?"

"They went to a lot of trouble to ensure Hecate's plans never came to fruition," I added.

Morgan turned her hands palms up. "I can't walk away. It would be wrong. Hecate suffered on my account. The least I can do is help."

"She's already free," Maeve said.

Morgan turned her mismatched gaze on the seer. "Since when?"

"Hard to pinpoint these events with precision, but at least four weeks."

"Then why hasn't she sought me out?" Pain lined Morgan's words, but she didn't need my pity.

"She was imprisoned for centuries," Maeve replied. "She must be quite weak. It will require time for her magic to reach a level where she can accomplish much of anything."

"Beyond that," I said, choosing my words carefully, "she paid a high price for creating you. Perhaps she—"

Morgan held up a hand. "Stop right there. You have no way of knowing anything."

I started to tell her she needed to look at all the possibilities, but she had such a desolate look on her face, I switched to, "You're absolutely correct."

"The other piece of information we unearthed is about a witch with two familiars," Maeve cut in.

"Second time today I heard about that one," Morgan muttered.

"How so?" Maeve asked.

"One of the Mer people told me she recalled lore about such a witch, except she couldn't recall quite what she'd read."

"Or perhaps she didn't want to discourage you." Maeve's voice was as gentle as I've ever heard it. A far cry from her drill sergeant imitation back in the library.

"Discourage me how?"

The seer stepped forward and placed a hand on Morgan's bare shoulder. "This news is not good, but it was penned by a psychic several hundred years ago, so it might not be accurate."

Morgan straightened. "Are you going to tell me? Or keep tossing caveats in the way?"

"The only thing I will impart is you must proceed with caution and measure your actions before jumping into something new."

I struggled to maintain a neutral expression. Damn it. Maeve wasn't going to tell her she would fail in her task, presumably reuniting with Hecate, and end up cursed because of it. Granted, the prophecy was vague. Cursed by whom came to mind. The world was a different place than it had been in the 1400s.

Very few foresights were set in stone.

"Is there anything else?" Morgan looked from Maeve to me.

"They came here to help us." Zeke woofed softly as he rebuked his mistress.

"I didn't kick them out." Morgan shut her eyes for a moment. When she opened them, she said, "Sorry. I'm tired. I have to do a test run to see how far my power will stretch teleporting. I can't do that with the animals. Maybe the two of you could remain here long enough for me to run an experiment."

Zeke kicked his head back and howled.

"Hush." Morgan wrapped a hand around his muzzle. "You're supposed to be an Australian shepherd."

The wolf quieted, but said, *"You are not leaving here without me."*

"Or me," Sita chirped.

"You'd be with Damien and Maeve—if they're amenable." Compulsion wove into Morgan's words, but the animals weren't swayed.

"Fine," she muttered. "I need sleep anyway."

Maeve nudged me, but I had no idea what she was getting at other than perhaps we'd overstayed our welcome.

I've always had a mulish side. Now that I was here, I wasn't leaving. Not unless Morgan forced me out—and maybe not even then. I could hover on the sidelines with the best of them.

"We'll leave you to it," I told Morgan. "Maeve will probably return to Faery. I'll rent another room here. When you're ready to leave, I'll come along to ensure you make it to your destination."

"But she shouldn't go at all," Maeve protested.

Morgan set her mouth in a tight line. "Goddess damn it. What did I do to be stuck with oversight? No one in the Coven ever watched my every move."

I grinned. "Told you before. I'm a hard guy to get rid of."

"This isn't your battle," Maeve reminded me.

"Your opinion, not mine," I shot back.

"*I want him with us,*" Zeke reminded her.

The wolf has always been my ally. I could have hugged him.

"Come back to Faery; we'll figure this out," Maeve invited.

Morgan shook her head. "The Fae have done too much for me already. Time for me to find my own path."

What lay behind her words? Tired of being put off, I pushed into her mind, trying for subtlety. Desolation, sorrow, fear for me cropped up before she whipped her head around.

"Stop that."

"It's instructive." I stepped closer, keeping my gaze on

her face rather than her cleavage. "You do not need to be afraid for me."

"I don't, huh? How about the time the Dearg Due nearly had you?"

I bristled. "I was solving that problem."

"Not what it looked like from my end." Breath hissed from between clenched teeth. "You've done a lot for me. Too much, actually. Time for me to test my new magic."

"What happens if it's not enough? You could get caught in a journey portal and not be able to get back. If Zeke and Sita are with you, they'll be trapped too. Eventually, something unpleasant will venture along and—"

"You can't know any of that," Morgan cut in.

"Of course, I can't, but it's an unnecessary risk. I can see you safely to anywhere."

She narrowed her eyes. "Do you promise to leave right after?"

"No. You'll still need a way back."

"What if I manage on my own without a bailout from you? Then, would you leave?"

I hesitated. What had changed from her cuddling in my arms after I'd hustled us out of the boardinghouse? She'd become progressively more distant since hunting for me after I was kidnapped by the Paranormal Detective Agency. Had it convinced her I couldn't take care of myself?

"We should leave," Maeve announced. "This is going nowhere."

I made shooing motions with one hand. "Go ahead. I'm staying."

Something flickered across Morgan's face, but it was

gone so quickly I couldn't interpret it. Was a tiny part of her relieved not to be alone?

Zeke licked my hand. Sita cooed happily.

Maeve tucked a hand around my elbow. "Outside. Now."

Before I could protest, she snagged me with a spell. When it cleared, we were on the outskirts of town in a thick grove of evergreens. Their boughs provided shelter from the incessant rain.

"You didn't have to do that," I sputtered.

"Aye, but I did." She squared off, facing me. "You're allowing your feelings for the witch to color your judgment."

"Guilty, but I'm not about to let her see if her magic stretches far enough to transport her and the two familiars across this country, the Atlantic, and all of Europe."

"It probably would. In many ways, she's far stronger than we are now."

I spun one hand in a get-on-with-it motion. "Probably isn't good enough. What happened to augment the magic she thought she was born with? Hecate hasn't been here to kindle the new version. No one has. Last I checked, power doesn't suddenly bloom brighter absent an intervention of great magnitude."

"I'm not sure. Bigger elements are in play here."

"What does that even mean? Don't give me more of your seer double talk, either."

I wasn't expecting an answer. Maeve wasn't in the habit of imparting information beyond bare-bones minimum.

She let go of my arm. "This is one instance where I truly do not have answers. Usually, I have multiple versions of possible futures. Not here. But there's this sense of foreboding"—she tapped her breastbone—"that won't lift. I have no idea where it's coming from."

"Morgan's in grave danger, right?"

Maeve nodded. "She has been ever since she sloughed her glamour and revealed herself to her Coven. What I can't figure out is why or what direction the danger is coming from. When I try to scry it, my ball turns black."

I drew back. "Is that common?"

"Never happened before. Red, yes. Black, no."

I'd seen her ball awash in red.

The ominous feeling that had been dogging me ever since Morgan left Faery returned in spades. "I'm going to get back there before she decides to leave without me."

Maeve's blue gaze drilled into me. "What will you do if she's already gone?"

"Follow her."

"Are there any words that will dissuade you?"

It was an odd question. "No. Why?"

The seer crossed her arms beneath her breasts. "Morgan is correct about one thing. This is not Fae business, but, if you persist, it will become so. Do you want to be the one who drags us into a war?"

"Have you seen that?"

"Not exactly," she hedged.

"Then what have you seen?"

"Already told you. Nothing definitive. My globe turns black."

I sifted through her words. She was leaving something

out, but I couldn't risk taking the time to determine exactly what.

"I'll be in touch when I can." Without waiting for another salvo from her, I covered the distance to the Motel 6 and checked in. The parking lot was filling with what I presumed were hookers and their johns. Better to have a room than not.

Once I had a key card for room 120, I walked to 114, stopped, and knocked. A quick scan told me she and the animals were still within; relief flooded through me like a warm tide.

"What is it now?"

"I'll be in room 120. Just wanted to let you know."

"You're wasting your time, Damien."

"Let me be the judge of that."

It was tough to walk away, but I did. My room was a clone of hers. I set a magical marker to alert me if she left and lay on the bed. I had my phone, but when I drew it from a pocket, the battery showed 20 percent. No cord, so I did what I could to shore it up with enchantment and started researching Hecate and her shrines in Turkey.

Despite Maeve's warning, I was exactly where I belonged. Morgan and I were destined to be together, no matter how long it took her to warm to the idea. Except she already had, and something soured her enthusiasm.

If I could pinpoint it, I could fix it.

Maybe.

She'd cared about me once. I'd felt it. And then I remembered the flicker of something when I'd announced I was staying. It encouraged me.

I can be charming and irresistible. And tenacious as fuck. I'd win her back, no matter what it took. I already had the wolf and hawk in my court. How tough could this be? She was all alone in the world, and—

Stop. Just stop, an inner voice piped up. Morgan had to want me for me, not because I was the only game in town.

I went back to my iPhone research and was deep into an arcane article about goddess worship when the marker I'd set to track Morgan blared a warning. On my feet in a trice, I bolted from the room determined to be so hot on her heels I'd catch up before she made a mistake.

A quick stop in front of 114 gave me what I needed to set a tracking spell in motion. Before I choked on my own hubris—maybe she didn't exactly need me—I crafted a spell and set off in pursuit.

CHAPTER NINE, MORGAN

I wasn't exactly surprised when Damien alerted me he and Maeve were nearby. Zeke had already told me as much. I'd dunned myself for not keeping closer watch. The wolf really likes Damien, which should reassure me, but it only makes keeping him at bay that much more difficult. It's finally sunk in I'm never going to have the kind of life where I can partner up with anyone beyond the animals.

Telling Damien no over and over was tough. Most of the time I wanted to melt into his arms and let him hold me. The physical attraction had done nothing but grow stronger. On the rare occasions when I actually slept, dreams of him naked and in my arms plagued me.

Maybe, if I hadn't been raised in a Coven that may as well have been a cloister, things might have been different. Witches aren't prudes, but neither were we allowed access to men. Many crossed the line, but always in deepest secrecy. Our programming was we didn't *need* men. They were superfluous and only got in the way of total concentration on our magic.

Damien wasn't raised with the same rule book. Even if he had been, I suspect it wouldn't have made any difference. I respected his independence and his courage, but it didn't mean I had time to invest in anything beyond Hecate and the role she'd created me for.

Zeke was ridiculously happy to see Damien. Sita too. Made it harder for me to pretend indifference while guarding my thoughts. A couple of times Maeve stared at me so hard I was certain she saw through to my bones, but she kept her own counsel.

I'm never sure how to read her other than she is on my side. Sort of. As much as a different type of magic-wielder can be. Damien threw down a gauntlet, said he was going to rent a room and stick to me like glue, but then Maeve dragged him off somewhere.

I considered leaving right then, but I was exhausted. Whether I commanded sufficient magic to get to Turkey, even if I took it in stages, remained to be seen, but I'd be a fool to tackle it if I weren't fresh. At first, I didn't think I could sleep, but I lay back down, shut my eyes, and focused on breathing.

Just breathing.

Damien's sharp-boned face, green eyes, and hunky body formed behind my closed lids. For once, I didn't chase the image away. Just drank him in, appreciating the sheer maleness of him. I wasn't surprised when he told me he was in a nearby room.

I'm not sure if I slept, but a few hours later I felt more

rested. Refreshed enough to embark on the first leg of a long journey. My clothes had mostly dried. I got back into them.

"What are we doing?" Zeke asked.

"Leaving."

"We can't go without Damien," Sita protested.

"We can and we are," I told the hawk. "If you'd rather remain with him, he's in room 120."

A couple of sharp beak claps suggested Mother's familiar wasn't pleased with me.

Zeke whined. I felt for him. Wolves are pack animals and, for whatever reason, he now included Damien as part of his pack. Once I'd finished dressing, I knelt in front of him.

"I'm sorry, but I need to do this alone. Not sure why I feel that way, but I do."

"Alone without me?" Zeke drew away.

"No, dear heart. Never without you or Sita." I flinched at the white lie. I'd been strongly considering this travel spell without them.

"So, alone means without Damien," Sita squawked and turned away from me.

I opened my mouth to ask why they were so all-fired certain he needed to be included, but shut it. The topic wasn't up for debate.

I've never raised a child, but the basic principles are the same. Families aren't democracies.

After one last look around the room to make certain I had everything, I summoned power. It danced to my command as if it had been waiting in the wings all along.

Encouraging.

Our next stop would be the East Coast, specifically the town of St. Johns in Newfoundland since it was closer to the UK than any other point in North America. It was winter, so I'd be underdressed, but I could purchase warmer clothing if my back was up against the wall.

For the few hours we laid over in St. Johns, a warm motel room would do the trick. I never had gotten anything to eat beyond the fare in the leather sack, but I'd remedy that once we arrived at our destination.

Sita flew to my shoulder, talons digging deep. Zeke was pouting too. Nothing for it but to loose my spell. We arrived in the blink of an eye, emerging into a damp, chilly evening. Much later here than on the West Coast. Not far from dawn. It worked in our favor.

No one saw us take shape from the ether.

I hastily draped a glamour over Zeke turning him back into an Aussie. My next move was a leash.

"*Not necessary,*" he huffed.

"It is if we meet anyone."

"*It's the middle of the night. They're all asleep.*"

"*Probably true, but better safe than sorry.*" I mirrored his mind speech in case anyone was about. Talking out loud to yourself is generally frowned upon no matter which culture prevails.

We were on the waterfront in a business district. Pay phones have gone the way of the Dodo bird, but I spied one and grabbed the phone book to hunt down a motel. I really did need a cell phone, but I could deal with it some other time. After I returned from Turkey. Besides, no shops would be open in the middle of the night.

Someone had ripped out a few pages of the phone book, but I located a couple of chain motels that looked promising and set a path for a Courtyard by Marriott. I wasn't at all sure if they took dogs—and they'd certainly frown on birds—so I told Zeke and Sita to wait for me at the edge of a vast parking lot.

A sleepy-eyed desk clerk checked me in. I had a rough moment when he asked for my passport but smothered him in compulsion and told him I'd misplaced it and would bring it round in the morning.

Key card in hand, I rounded up the animals, draped them in invisibility, and marched us through the lobby and up the elevator to the fourth floor.

Our room was much nicer than Motel 6 had been. Interesting because this one only cost ten bucks more a night. Two queen beds were smothered in pillows and luxe down comforters. The bathroom had granite counters and a fancy showerhead with multiple settings. A tempting basket of soaps and shampoos graced the counter. Besides a television, the room also had a refrigerator and a microwave.

Zeke jumped onto one of the beds, leaving a trail of muddy footprints.

Oh-oh. He was in such a mood, I didn't tell him to get down, merely scattered magic to obliterate his tracks so Clara Hilton—my faux identity—didn't end up blacklisted throughout the Marriott chain.

A room service menu jumped out at me. According to it, the kitchen was open 24/7. I ordered a hamburger for Zeke, a cobb salad and French bread for me, and a bowl of granola for Sita with milk on the side. The kitchen must not have been busy because the food showed up in less than a quarter hour. I'd stashed the animals in the bathroom in anticipation of a waiter showing up, but I'd barely closed the door when he knocked.

Once he left, I sealed the sill with locks and magic, invited Zeke and Sita to join me, and dug in. We'd no sooner begun eating than the telltale feel of Damien's magic jolted me.

He oozed through a portal and into the room. "Oooh, dinner. Mind if I share?"

I tried. Goddess knows, I tried, but a giggle escaped, followed by another. Moments later, I was laughing uproariously.

"Hush, you'll wake your neighbors," Damien murmured. "What's so funny?"

"You," I managed between gales of laughter. Took me a while to mute my outburst.

"Why?" He arched a pale brow.

No one has a right to be that gorgeous. My heartbeat escalated, and my throat thickened with wanting him. "I cannot believe how persistent you are."

A shrug. "Told you that the first night we met—or shortly thereafter. Tough to shake me if I don't want to leave."

The animals had mobbed him. Zeke still had his paws on his shoulders, and Sita flew around the room shrieking like a mad thing.

"Quiet," I told the hawk. "Damien is right."

Zeke jumped down after an effusive tongue bath.

Damien waltzed over to my salad and scooped a couple bits of bacon off the top, popping them into his mouth.

"We could order you something," I said. "Service is quick."

"It would be at four a.m."

"Do you want something?" I persisted.

"Depends. Do you plan to eat the whole salad?"

I nodded.

"Then, yes." He spied the menu I'd discarded and glanced at it. "This." He pointed. "A cup of tea and a piece of berry pie."

I snorted, picked up the phone, and ordered. "They're going to think I'm auditioning for *My 600-Pound Life*."

"Never heard of it, but then watching television has always been low on my list."

I shooed the animals back into the bathroom. "You should join them," I told Damien.

"What? You're not allowed company in a room you paid for?"

My cheeks grew warm, as I turned beet-red.

"It's okay." He edged toward the bathroom door. "Come close so we can talk while we wait."

"What about?" I followed him until I stood beneath the lintel.

"How'd getting here go?"

"Almost too simple. If it's a bellwether, I could make it to Europe easily."

"Did anything appear out of place?"

It was an odd question, so I recreated my journey from when we'd left Motel 6. "The only quirk was how quickly we got here. It couldn't have taken more than a minute or two."

His eyes widened, shading to a deeper mossy shade. "Is your power still expanding?"

I hadn't considered that possibility. "Maybe. Not sure."

Stepping back a pace, I stilled my racing heart. Being this close to Damien was dangerous territory. I'd been about to stroke his shoulder, pushing stray hairs behind it.

A brisk knock saved me from myself. After shoving the bathroom door closed, I hurried to let the waiter in, except it wasn't a hotel employee with a cart pushing into my room.

Two witches barreled inside and kicked the door shut. They could have been twins with cropped dark hair shot with silver and dark eyes. Black robes sashed in red covered their tall, skinny bodies.

One grabbed me and deployed a sound shield. "Finally. Got you, you slimy piece of shit."

"Your Coven will pay handsomely for your return," the other smirked.

Great. They'd issued a bounty for my capture. Why hadn't I foreseen it?

I hissed and spat and twisted to escape the first witch's grip. Last time I'd gone toe-to-toe with the sisterhood, I'd ended up killing five of them. Made me cautious about raising magic to end this.

Were more witches waiting outside? Easy to find out. I sent a seeking spell arcing outward and located three more in the parking lot. Made sense. Odd numbers hold power.

"Let go of me," I snapped.

"Fat fucking chance," the one hanging onto me growled.

A spell wound around me, hot and prickly. I had to blast through before it circled me completely, or they'd suck the consciousness right out of me. I knew this particular casting well.

A second knock suggested food had arrived.

The witch who had me in a death grip called, "Just leave whatever it is outside, sweetie, and put it on my room tab."

"You got it," the server replied. Footsteps thudded on the carpeted hall as he retreated.

"No time for you to eat it anyway," the other witch informed me.

Once again, the insidious entrapment spell was growing. I summoned power of my own while I still could. I'd given this a fair chance. If I killed them by accident, I'd deal with the fallout later. Besides, reinforcements lurked in my bathroom. The witches knew about Zeke, and maybe Sita, but they hadn't reckoned I'd partner with a Fae.

Or maybe they had after Mother's rescue.

What they knew—or didn't—scarcely mattered. A focused blast of destruction blew through the entrapment spell.

Zeke bounded across the room, knocking into the witch who held onto me and driving her to the floor where he stood over her snarling.

Sita latched onto the other witch, pecking hard enough to draw blood from multiple spots.

Damien strode after them, arms swinging, fists clenched. "It's in your best interest to leave and not return. Includes the bitches outside next to that black van." He punched the witch Sita clung to hard enough I heard bones crack. Blood shot from the ruins of what had been her nose.

The witch under Zeke tried to get up. He closed his jaws around her upper arm and bit hard.

"Don't you want a better bondmate?" she wheezed. "A real witch who can give you what's due such a magnificent creature?"

He bit her again.

"Told you the wolf was a lost cause," the other witch muttered as she batted at the hawk and did her damnedest to protect her head. Blood flowed onto the carpet.

Damien kicked the other witch in the ribs. Power crackled from his fingertips. Golden ropes slithered out of the air and wrapped around both witches. Whoa. Magical to the nines, one slid right through Zeke on its way to the witch trapped beneath him.

"Fuck it," I growled. "This is too much trouble. I'll kill them and be done with it."

"What about the other three?" Damien countered. "And the rest of the Coven hot on their heels once they sense this batch are dead?"

"We can't die," one sputtered.

Fury beat a track through me. What kind of emergency broadcast had my original Coven promulgated? I was starting to feel like the outlaw on Old West wanted posters.

"Oh yeah? Want to try me?" I made a grab for the one trying to evade Sita, gripped her upper arm, and sent a thread of magic straight to her throat.

She gagged and moved her hands from the sides of her

head to her airway, the passage I was closing off. Her eyes widened.

"Stop. We'll leave," she rasped, still clutching her throat. Color drained from her face. Blood flowed from her broken nose and all the places Sita had pecked her.

"I will stop. For now," I told her. "Just remember, you invaded my territory. Your life is in my hands."

"You killed my mistress," the hawk squawked and buried her beak in the witch's eye. "Death is too good for you."

A pain-saturated howl filled the room.

I deepened the sound shield around us. A day late and a dollar short, but I didn't want witnesses to further conversation.

Damien spoke words in Gaelic. The ropes tightened until both witches were trussed like the pigs they were.

"Zeke, to me."

The wolf rolled off his captive and ambled to my side.

"The ropes will cut off telepathy too," Damien informed me.

The esteem I felt for him edged up a few notches.

He stepped between the women. "You have a couple of choices. Return to the others outside, leave, and do not return."

"Call off the manhunt for me," I added. "Do it the same way it was initiated: through our internal communications network."

"Or?" The witch nearest me choked out.

I glanced Damien's way. He nodded imperceptibly.

"Or I'll mow through the five of you and any other

sisters stupid enough to track me down." I rolled my shoulders back. "I am Hecate's chosen, created with her essence. Stopping me will prove as impossible as holding back the tides."

"Created for what purpose?" the other witch wheezed.

"To ensure the sisterhood doesn't fall to darkness. It's already made significant inroads."

"Not possible," she retorted.

"Isn't it?" Damien stepped in. "Our seer has seen much. None of it is promising for your kind."

"Hell, Lilith, our Coven seer, knew the same thing," I added. "She'd already been turned, so her prophecies were tainted."

"You blaspheme. May Hecate flay your cursed hide," the witch Zeke had bitten groaned.

Interesting. Some of the sisterhood still worship her.

"We'll see who blasphemes." Damien nudged her with his boot. "Decision time. My supper is in the hall, and it's growing cold."

"We'll leave," one muttered.

"If you return"—I hunkered down and made eye contact—"no second chances. I will merrily make short work of any and all of you. Is that understood?"

"Untie us," the other said. It sounded far too much like a demand for my taste.

"Hell no." Damien snorted. "We'll teleport you back to your kinswomen outside."

"This had better be the end of it," I reminded them.

"We're not responsible for other Covens," the first witch said.

"You could be," I said. "Call off the hunt."

"Not sure we can."

I gave her points for honesty but not much else.

Damien conjured a spell; I added to it. When it hit velocity, the witches shimmered and vanished.

"What about your ropes?" I asked.

"Once they get far enough away from me, they'll dissipate." A knowing smile curved his chiseled lips. "They'll blow through scads of magic trying to defeat them in the meantime."

I grinned back. "You're creative."

"You should have killed them," Sita cawed.

Damien opened the door and retrieved the rolling cart. "Shall we?" he suggested. "Your meal is virtually untouched, and we want to leave before they call out the cavalry."

I sealed the door with spells, which might act as a deterrent, and sat near my salad. "But I told them not to."

"They won't listen. Not now, and not until Hecate shows up and slays a few." He settled next to me and removed a stainless steel lid from his prime rib dinner.

I appreciated his optimism, but I didn't believe the witch goddess would ever step forward to claim me.

"We could have done that. Slain a few." Sita was at it again.

Zeke nosed through to his hamburger, pushed the bun aside, and swallowed the meat patty whole. *"I want two more."* He nudged me.

"You can hunt later. I really don't want to bother room service again."

"Why not?" He pricked his ears forward.

"It draws attention to us."

Damien tossed him a chunk of fat. Zeke took up residence right in front of him, staring hopefully at the slab of meat.

Once I began eating, I realized how famished I was. When I finally came up for air after my plate was nearly empty, I said, "You've accomplished the impossible."

"How so?" Damien stopped with his fork midway to his mouth.

"I'm done telling you to go away."

Zeke woofed. Sita raised her beak from the nuts and seeds in the granola bowl and clacked it approvingly.

A rakish grin transformed Damien's features into something profanely beautiful. After setting his fork down, he wrapped his arms around me and settled his mouth atop mine.

CHAPTER TEN, DAMIEN

I probably shouldn't have kissed Morgan, but she was so close her spicy scent and mystical allure drove everything else from my mind. Cinnamon, vanilla, and mint swirled around us. The press of her lips against mine all but drove me mad. Between wanting her and pushing my desire to a distant back burner, I'd created my own special hell.

After a brief hesitation, she returned my embrace and gripped my shoulders as she snaked her tongue inside my mouth. I wasn't the only one who'd been sublimating desire. We'd kissed before, but there'd always been a barrier on her side, an ambivalence.

It wasn't there anymore as she pressed her body close. Nipples hardened when her breasts rubbed my chest. I twined my fingers through the silk of her hair and plunged my tongue inside her mouth. My cock shot to attention.

Our breath quickened as our tongues sparred.

Too much clothing.

She twisted in my arms, moaning softly as she tugged my shirt out of my trousers and slid a hand up my back, fingertips playing over ribs and shoulders. Next she teased the points of my ears.

I wanted her, but not like this. Not where we'd have to be damned quick and watchful all at the same time. Reluctantly, I drew back, broke our kiss, and then brushed her forehead, cheeks, and chin with my lips.

Cupping the side of her face in my hand, I murmured, "You are the most incredible, amazing, lissome creature, but I want our first time to be special, not rushed and sandwiched in between worries."

The words were no sooner out than I shook my head. "That didn't come out right."

Her beautiful lips were swollen from our extended kiss. "Which part?"

My errant member throbbed in time with my erratic heartbeat. The combination made it difficult to think or find words. "The one that made me sound like a hopeless romantic. Normally, I'd scoop you up and carry you to one of those inviting beds, but we have to leave. Sooner the better. Before every Coven in Eastern Canada converges on us. Probably shouldn't have taken time to eat, but the food was already here."

Her mismatched gaze had softened with passion. "Surely a few minutes one way or the other won't matter." For the barest moment, she rested a hand over the bulge in my pants.

I ran my thumb over the seam of her lips. "I don't want a

mere few minutes with you, Morgan. Even our immorality isn't long enough to worship every nuance, every secret of your amazing body. Our time will come, but it's not here or now."

She nodded. "I suppose you're right." Half a grin lightened her features. "I was so taken by your considerable charms, I forgot about everything else."

"Me too. We'll carve out time when the sisterhood isn't hot on our heels."

"Will that ever happen?" Wistfulness underlined her words.

"Of course." I gathered her close and stroked her hair. Loving her near me vied with an increasing sense we were living on borrowed time.

Finally, I let go. "If you have anything here, grab it. Something isn't right." I turned to my plate, intent on one more bite before I drew a transport spell together, only to find it empty.

Zeke trained innocent eyes on me. *"You left it."*

I laughed softly. "So I did. Glad someone got the benefit."

"You ate Damien's dinner?" Morgan stood over her familiar and shook a finger at him before shrugging into her jacket and grabbing the sack Logan had gifted her.

"It's all right. Join your power with mine. Something's heading our way. We must be gone from here."

Zeke stood on one side of me. Sita flew to Morgan's shoulder. Her magic sought my casting and joined it. Our power slotted nicely together. Different iterations of mage rarely work in tandem. But we did.

The hotel room flickered and gave way to the dark of a journey channel. Next to me, Morgan shuddered.

"What is it?" I asked.

"We left in the nick of time. Witches are pouring into the room. They were cloaked. Until they weren't. How come you sensed them when I couldn't?"

"It was more intuition than anything specific. They almost had to come back."

"Guess they didn't believe me when I said I'd kill them."

"Why would they?" I countered. "Immortals don't think in those terms."

"My world is so different I can't even absorb how it operates most days."

Compassion flooded me, but it wasn't helpful. Morgan would need every iota of strength in the coming days, weeks, and probably months. Her world had tipped upside down, and it wasn't about to tip back.

The edges of my spell took on a glowing aspect. We were nearly to my chosen destination. I'd picked a crumbling crypt in a graveyard on the outskirts of Carlisle in Northern England because it was a spot I knew. We required more research before we emerged in Turkey.

The smells of mold and faint rot surrounded us as my spell dissipated.

"Where are we?" Morgan asked. "This can't be Turkey. Too cold and humid."

"We're north of Carlisle. Thought we'd go to ground here long enough to pinpoint our target in Turkey."

"*No one out there,*" Zeke told us.

Steps leading through the crypt to the outside were in

far worse shape than when I'd last been here a couple of hundred years earlier. Big surprise. Zeke turned into the brown dog he'd been when I first met him as we clomped up the stairs single file and into twilight shading to evening. Days are short in this part of the world this time of year.

The graveyard was wet and muddy. We made our way across it to a roadway. I tugged my cell phone from an inner pocket and tapped the display a few times to bring international usage online.

"I need one of those." Morgan nudged me.

"Not a problem now you have both funds and ID." I scrolled through Safari hunting for an inn where we could hole up for the night. I'd masked our travel spell. Hopefully, it would buy us a few uninterrupted hours to research Hecate's shrine in Lagina in the Caria portion of southwestern Turkey.

I prefer to be prepared. Just popping out there could be dangerous, particularly if Maeve was correct about Hecate being free. For all I knew, she'd be so furious about her long imprisonment, she'd be plotting to snuff out Morgan once and for all because of all the trouble her making had caused.

No. We had to proceed carefully. Perhaps starting in a neighboring region where we could procure Eastern garb so we'd blend in more readily.

"Found a couple of places that are close by," I said. "Let me call to see if we can get a room."

Morgan nodded. Her mind felt busy to me, but she wasn't inclined to say much.

Half an hour later, we were checked in at a small bed and breakfast establishment that allowed dogs—for twenty quid extra. Sita waited in a nearby tree. She'd fly through a window once we told her which one.

Unlike the cookie-cutter room at the Marriott, this tiny chamber tucked under the eaves of a four-story Victorian, had one double bed piled high with pillows, a clawfoot tub, and antique furniture. The floor was shiny wood that had been polished to within an inch of its life.

I pushed up the sash, undid the screen, and called Sita. She flew into the room ruffling her feathers as she perched on the edge of an armoire.

Here we were in one more hotel room, but neither of us seemed inclined to pick up where we'd left off in St. Johns. Morgan still wore a worried look. She'd settled on the room's only chair tucked beneath a small table.

"What's worrying you?" I asked. Better to get these things out in the open.

"What isn't?" She shut her eyes for a moment. "It took me a while to process this, but that one witch said I was cursed. She also cursed me. You cannot take something like that back. It will hang over my head forever."

"But it was just words," I protested.

"You don't get it. The worst thing that can happen to anyone is being cursed by a witch. It means you'll live under a cloud forever." She closed her teeth over her lower lip. "It's kind of like carrying around a hex bag you can never get shut of."

I picked my words carefully. "Surely, there's a counter spell. Most castings have them."

"Not this one." She dropped her head into her hands. "We may as well go back to Faery. It's maybe the only place I'll be safe." She straightened. "What am I saying. You should return to Faery. All I'll do is bring the wrath of the gods down on the Fae. No point in trying to find Hecate. I've been marked. I won't be any good to her now."

"Can she countermand the curse?"

A shrug. "I have no idea."

Riding on a hunch, I knelt in front of her and grasped a hand. "You miss the sisterhood. It's all you've known virtually your entire life. What happened to you would be like Faery being pulled out from under me. Except, in your case, things keep getting worse. First your Coven exiled you, and now other witches have cursed you."

"I understand full well what happened to me. What's your point?" She dragged her hand out of mine.

"There must have been aspects of life in the Coven that grated." I hesitated before adding, "There's an old saying. Freedom's just another word for nothing left to lose."

"I know that song. So what?"

"When you get past the shock of rejection, there's got to be an empowering aspect to being your own witch. Not under anyone's thumb. Not bound by rules you thought were ridiculous."

A fractured sigh stuttered past her lips. "You're trying to make me feel better. I appreciate it, but maybe Zeke and I should vanish. Start over where no one knows us and pretend we're just a woman and her dog."

"What about me?" Sita shrilled.

Morgan got up and walked to the hawk. "I'm bad news. You're better off with Damien and Maeve in Faery."

Sita puffed out her feathers. "Not what Zoelle would have wanted."

"Mother would have wanted you to be safe," Morgan murmured.

"I'm responsible for my own choices, and I will remain by your side. I'm here for a reason. You need me."

"Same goes for me," I said. "None of us are going anywhere. I say we stick with the game plan and find Hecate."

"Maeve didn't think it was a good idea at all."

"I'm not her, and I don't always agree with her conclusions even if she does have inside information."

"Every witch will be on high alert hunting for us," Morgan pointed out. "This isn't fair to you."

"None of this is fair, not to you, either. What happened to not telling me to get lost?"

She set her mouth in a tight line. "That was before the whole curse thing."

In my cursory research about witches, the topic of witchy curses hadn't reared its head. I missed the Fae library; I'd relied heavily on its bounty. We kept a manor house in the Highlands. Perhaps I could finesse a side trip while Morgan rested. They had their own collection of scrolls, though not nearly as extensive an array.

"How about this?" I suggested and handed over my phone. "Find out what you can about Lagina."

She sent a pointed glance my way. "What will you be doing?"

I grinned. "Och, ye know me far too well."

"Drop the Gaelic and answer my question."

"Who would have guessed such beauty could mask a taskmistress?" I teased.

Her tormented expression, brows like broken bird's wings, softened. "Sorry. Not trying to be a bitch."

"I'm going to pay a quick visit to our stronghold in the Highlands to research witch curses."

She turned her hands palms up. "Why bother? You have me."

"Is it possible you missed something? We must be thorough. I shouldn't be gone more than a couple of hours."

"Sure. Okay. I'll cloak us the moment you leave."

Bending, I kissed the top of her head. "Do not answer the door, no matter what. I'll teleport in and out of here."

"Got it." Rising to her feet, she wrapped her arms around me. "You really should absorb your losses and get out while you can."

"Not my style. What kind of Fae would I be if I cut and ran at the first hint of problems?"

I wanted to kiss her, but if I did, I might not leave. We couldn't remain here much past checkout time tomorrow, and I had a lot of ground to cover.

Disentangling her arms, I murmured, "Back soon," and set a course for a crumbling castle outside Thurso on the northern tip of Scotland.

BACK IN THE DAY, all our domiciles led straight into Faery. No longer. None of us are sure why that is. Perhaps Faery's inherent enchantment has dimmed in the face of a world where mortals no longer believe in magic.

Regardless, one gateway after another closed until the only physical route into my ancestral land was the veils I'd brought Morgan through. Of course, all Fae can teleport in and out, but I did not want to burn through that level of power. If we continued to run up against roadblocks, I'd need every scrap of magic at my beck and call.

The smell of moss on ancient rocks brought memories flooding back. I'd lived here for a while back in the 1300s. And then again in the 1500s. My boots made a hollow thumping sound as I hurried along deserted corridors toward where the library used to be.

Where was everyone?

A cursory scan revealed a few Fae, but on the lower levels of the manor house. Probably a good thing. I didn't exactly have time to sing "Aude Lang Syne" and catch up. The musty scent of ancient vellum was reassuring. Probably much like in Faery, no one frequented this library, either.

I crossed beneath the lintel and told the room to deliver whatever it possessed concerning witches and curses. I'd expected a flood of source documents. Two scrolls plopped onto the table. Surely, there'd be more. Nope, only the two. I dragged out a chair, sat, and pulled the nearest scroll close.

I was midway through it before it sank in that these were the only ones meeting my stringent requirements. Scanning, I worked my way through the scroll in front of me. It basically said what Morgan had: witch curses were forever. Whoever had penned this missive thought it far better to avoid witches entirely.

Disappointed, I pushed it aside and unrolled the second scroll. The vellum crumbled beneath my touch, so I patched the broken places with a spot of magic. Information was far more detailed here. Medea and Circe had been sorceresses before signing on as Hecate's apprentices.

The three had recognized witch magic as different from the ability possessed by other iterations of magic wielder.

Interesting. I hadn't heard that theory before.

Bending closer, I kept reading. Apparently, witches could bend the four elements together in such a way that whatever end point they envisioned would become permanent if they breathed life into their casting.

I puzzled over a passage written in a form of Gaelic even more ancient than the earlier part of the scroll. Wanting to be certain of its meaning, I pushed to my feet and made my way to an enormous dictionary located on a stand. Each of our libraries has one. Once there, I proceeded to look up words.

The upshot was witch spells could be permanent, but it applied to all their spells, not curses specifically.

"Thought I sensed you," a male voice called from the direction of the hall.

I twisted to face the door.

Tobias, one of the elder Fae, swished into the room. Not much over five feet tall, he wore a brilliant red silk robe sashed in cream. Golden curls fell to shoulder level. Hazel eyes that missed very little zeroed in on me; the points of his ears twitched.

I grinned and covered the distance between us, hands

extended. He clasped them. "It's been too long," I murmured.

"I rarely leave these days," he explained. "Everything I need is here."

"Don't you miss Faery?"

A wistful expression sharpened his angular features. "Of course. I communicate with Maeve, Bess, and Zoe regularly."

I let go of his hands. "I'd almost forgotten. You're a seer too."

He nodded. "Aye, and my visions told me you'd be here."

"What else did they say?" I sucked in a breath. Would he be more forthcoming than Maeve?

"Come." He gestured at the table. "Sit. We shall talk for a while."

I started to say not for too long, but didn't. If he had information, I'd remain until I heard everything.

We settled across from one another. A tray laden with afternoon tea pastries and fruit floated into the room and landed between us followed by a second tray with a teapot and cups.

"It's rare I get company," he commented as he poured tea for us.

I waited. I've been dealing with seers long enough to understand nothing I asked would hurry him along.

"You hooked up with a witch, but not just any witch. Nay, this one stands in the center of a maelstrom." He speared me with his gaze. "Why not return to Faery. Let the witch fight her own battles. There will be many. In truth, I could not find an end to them."

Hmmm. The *give up and go home* message was growing old.

No reason to hide anything from Tobias, so I kept it simple. "I love her. Our paths crossed for a reason. It wasn't accidental."

"No arguments on that." He chuckled. "In love, eh. After all these years with all the Fae you could have partnered with, you chose a witch."

His statement didn't require an answer, so I asked, "Do you know if we will actually find Hecate?"

"She's free, so the odds are good. She will not take kindly to you, though. She sees the witch as her creature."

I spun one hand in a get-on-with-it gesture.

He shook his index finger back and forth. "None of that."

"Morgan is convinced she's cursed because of what a witch who came after us said. Will it make any difference?"

He cocked his head to one side. "Depends what type of difference you're hoping for. From what I've gathered, Hecate's original plans were foiled by her fellow gods and goddesses. They'll give you more grief than Hecate because she wants revenge. If what I've seen is accurate, she will use any and every game piece at her disposal to rain destruction on those who crossed her.

"The witch she made with her own essence could be a powerful element."

"Morgan will never allow herself to be used," I said.

"I wondered about that. If she isn't biddable, Hecate will have no use for her."

"What about her original plan to root out evil in the covens?"

"It may have fallen by the wayside. Avenging wrongs can be all-consuming." He slapped a palm on the table. "Regardless, there is no space for a Fae in the mix. Best case scenario, she'll tell you to leave. Worst, she'll make your life miserable for pairing up with her minion."

"Have you actually seen that?"

Fae cannot lie. We can hold silence, but we cannot twist the truth.

"Not exactly," Tobias admitted. "I'm extrapolating from the things I do know."

"Morgan is convinced she's cursed, that she's no good to anyone."

He arched a fair brow. "Have you considered returning to Faery? Both of you."

I gathered my thoughts before I answered him. "Aye, but if we do, Morgan will be plagued with might-have-beens for all the long years of her life. This thing, whatever it is, needs to play itself out."

"You really do love her," he murmured.

"I do. When next you talk with Maeve, please tell her you saw me and that we're okay."

"I will." He drained his teacup and rose. "If you can, stop in on your way back. I've always enjoyed your company."

I got to my feet too. "And I yours. I'll return if I can."

"Be careful, Damien. Mages who tamper with the workings of the gods almost always regret it."

One moment he stood in front of me, the next he was gone. I instructed the scrolls to find their places. The passage I'd been trying to translate might have been written about Morgan. It said:

With two familiars, I am unique among witches.

Curse me once, I may sink.

Curse me again, I will rise above you and make you pay.

Do not trifle with my magic. Strong and vibrant, it will salvage all wrongs.

The phrase looked promising on its surface, but, like all prophecies, thorns lurked amid its petals. The sinking part was particularly problematic.

I'd accomplished all I could here. Past time to return. The pastries were untouched. I wrapped them in a napkin to bring with me. Visualizing the cozy bed and breakfast in Carlisle, I loosed my spell.

Perhaps the manor house offered an assist. Seconds later, I walked through a portal and into an empty chamber.

My chest tightened. The napkin with its bounty dropped onto the floor. What the unholy hell? I'd told Morgan to stay put. Nothing was out of place. No sign of a struggle, but she was gone along with Zeke and Sita.

She'd promised she was done with her arcane cat and mouse game.

The empty room mocked me. I shaped the remains of my teleport spell into a tracking one but stopped before sending it forth.

Did I really want to chase her down again?

Eh, I wasn't thinking straight. Nope. I was reacting because my pride just took it up the shorts. Bending, I retrieved a croissant, dusted it off, and stuffed it into my mouth.

A faint ping led me to my phone. She'd left it next to the bed. I picked it up, hoping for a text or a note or a voice message. None of the above. I pushed my nascent casting into the world before its velocity waned. And then I pushed harder seeking her location.

Nothing.

I'm one of the best trackers the Fae have ever spawned, but I had no idea where she'd gone. How could that be? Only a couple of hours had elapsed. Even if she'd gone off-world, my ability would have pinpointed her location.

I dragged out the crystal Maeve had gifted me, the one paired to a twin in Morgan's possession. I let the stone warm in my hand and reached for her through its power.

Again. Nothing. I stared at the crystal, but its inner light was dim. Made sense if Morgan wasn't receiving my communication. Riding on a whim, I tugged the armoire open. The sack with Morgan's ID, money, and credit cards sat on the closet floor. When I picked it up, her crystal lay at the bottom.

Explained why she didn't answer.

Worried, but uncertain of my next steps, I paced from one end of the small chamber to the next and back again until logic prevailed. Instead of seeking Morgan, I tuned my tracking spell to Zeke.

Bingo.

The wolf was indeed off-world in somewhere dark, foreboding. Maybe a cave or a mineshaft. I couldn't tell from this distance, but it bore a passing resemblance to one of Maeve's visions.

If Morgan had cast a concealment spell, she'd have included the hawk and wolf. It led me to suspect someone else was involved. They'd masked Morgan, not bothering with the animals.

It decided me, but I'd have to be stealthy. If Morgan was in trouble and I plopped down out of nowhere, I'd likely end up trapped too.

After blending my essence with Earth's, I followed cautiously, alert for booby traps in the travel channel. I'm vulnerable at transition points where my castings begin and end. Having made it to the far side of my spell—underground somewhere—I cinched up the talent anchoring invisibility and traced Morgan's unique energy.

Unlike when I'd searched from the hotel room, I sensed her here and hurried forward.

CHAPTER ELEVEN, MORGAN

I was rested—more or less—and we'd just eaten. Nothing to do but wait for Damien's return. He'd left me his phone and password, so I dug into Safari's database to find out more about Lagina and Hecate's shrine.

The shrine had been built in the second century of the Christian era in Corinthian fashion with eight columns on its shorter side and eleven on the longer one. Apparently, the Catholic Church owned the site now. I cringed. No wonder Hecate had abandoned it—if she'd actually ever spent much time there.

No love lost between witchcraft and modern religion.

The Mer regent suggested Hecate had been imprisoned in a cave beneath Lagina. I wondered about that. Whoever was responsible for sequestering her would have held the location close. In other words, no one would know where the witch goddess was except those who'd placed her there.

Perhaps Lagina was a false lead deliberately propagated to turn attention away from her real hiding spot.

No way to know without going there and checking. It would be a waste of time and magic if it were a dead end, but we had to start somewhere. Even with her free, there'd be traces of her if she'd been there recently. And tracking her might be possible.

I checked the time. Damien had been gone for an hour.

Back to mapping out a game plan. We'd definitely start in Lagina. If we didn't find a trace of Hecate anywhere close, we'd hatch up plan B. Hecate had to be more or less recovered by now. Why hadn't she made a point of looking for me?

It would make my life so much simpler.

I typed various possibilities into the phone's browser but didn't come up with any further clues about Hecate's domicile. But then, why would I? The Internet is only as good as whoever inputs data. No one who truly knew much about the gods and goddesses would have wanted mortals to share that information. Ergo, nothing beyond urban legends popped up.

My mind backtracked to the curse. Was I truly cursed? Or had her words been empty rhetoric? I checked my aura, my magical center, and proximity to my physical being hunting for a lurking darkness but found nothing.

Part of me was grateful, another part confused. If I were truly cursed, there'd have to be objective evidence. Did the fact I couldn't locate any mean I wasn't cursed or merely that I hadn't dug deep enough.

Zeke and Sita snoozed beneath a window. I squelched a

smile. Ever opportunistic, Zeke hadn't missed a beat when it came to half a slab of prime rib sitting unguarded within easy reach. Hard to blame him. He'd told me back in St. Johns he was still hungry.

Was I doing the right thing going in search of Hecate? She wasn't busting her butt to find me.

Would my time be better spent executing revenge for Mother's murder and my ouster from the Coven?

No reason I couldn't do both.

I didn't think it would work, but I raised my mind voice and called Damien. He didn't reply. Probably, he was too far away. Or maybe Fae enchantment blocked outside communication from wherever their enclave was. He'd never disclosed its location, but then I hadn't asked, either.

Damien.

When I shut my eyes, the touch of his lips, body crushed against mine came racing back. My breath quickened. The bulge in his trousers had been tantalizing, inviting. Would we ever find a private moment to explore one another's bodies?

I closed my teeth over my lower lip. Somehow, I'd moved from being convinced I didn't need him in my life to embracing the possibilities. How had it happened so quickly? Had he ensorcelled me?

No. He wouldn't have done that. When he'd been disappointed about my lack of enthusiasm for the Fae mating ceremony, he hadn't tried to coerce me with spells. Instead, he'd walked away. He was decent, not underhanded or unprincipled.

Wanting him clawed at me. I wasn't used to ignoring

lust. All it would take was a little rubbing, and I'd dissolve in a mind-bending orgasm. Except that wouldn't be the end of it. I'd still long for him. I rocked in my chair. Where my labia pressed together, liquid slicked them. My nipples hardened. The spicy scent of my arousal wafted through the room.

My fingers found their way between my legs.

That decided it. I moved from my chair to the bathroom seeking a shred of privacy. Not that Zeke or Sita would bat an eye, but I wasn't comfortable bringing myself off in front of anyone.

I turned on the shower to create a noise diversion, closed the commode, and sat on its lid. Suddenly, I couldn't wait. In a quick motion, I unzipped my pants without bothering to take them off. It would take longer to undress than to finish this so I could think again. Damien's body hovered behind my closed lids. Not that I'd seen him totally naked, but I'm a damn good improvisor. I sank one hand between my legs. With my other, I pinched my nipples and settled in to teasing my distended clit. My panties were a swamp. The musky scent of aroused witch, fiery and pungent, urged me on.

The teasing part didn't last long before I rubbed harder, faster, just the way I like it. I was panting now, lust spiraling as a series of orgasms roared through me. I'd figured one would do it, but my fingers had a mind of their own. They kept on keeping on until I was sucking air like a bellows.

So much for my secret trip to the john. I may as well have announced my intentions to the world before retiring behind a closed door. Once my breathing was starting to normalize, I turned off the shower, set myself to rights, rinsed my hands, and opened the door to the bedroom.

Damien should be back soon. Maybe I could air the place out somehow before—

I stared at the spot where I'd left Zeke and Sita. It was empty.

Clearly, they weren't anywhere in the room. My heart leapt into hyperdrive, but for entirely different reasons.

I felt for my link to the wolf. It was there—but not. Something stood between my magic and Zeke.

Fuck. I slammed a fist down on the table.

What in the hell happened while I was indulging myself?

Someone must have been watching us. No question about it, since they'd timed their move to coincide with my absence. I snatched my jacket and barreled out of the room intent on locating my wolf and the hawk.

Zeke would never go down without a hell of a fight.

I was so furious with myself for leaving my familiars alone, I barely remembered to pull the door shut. I left the key card in the room, but it didn't matter. There's never been a lock I couldn't open.

Dawn wasn't far off. The night was still, clear, chilly, and damp. Vintage England. I kept a line to Zeke open. I wasn't linked to Sita—or I didn't think I was. Now might be a good time to find out, so I set a tracking spell in motion to locate the hawk.

It bounced back in my face much as my hunt for Zeke had.

Goddess damn it to hell.

Zeke was my heart, my life. He's been part of me since I was a small child. He couldn't be gone. No way. My stomach twisted into a painful knot. Bile splashed the back of my throat.

I dashed this way and that, urging my tracking magic to yield something. Anything.

Reason intruded, barely. I should wait for Damien. Beyond waiting, I should be cautious. Whatever nabbed my beasts had to be lurking. A trap with my name on it could be closing in. No way someone would target Zeke and Sita and leave me alone.

Sometimes I'm slow on the uptake, but I wound layers of warding around myself. Made it tougher to keep my tracking spells active, but I couldn't do my familiars any good if I went down too.

What to do? I flirted with going back inside and leaving Damien a note, but if he could read it so could anyone else. Ditto for runes. Where was he? I tried calling him again.

I hadn't expected an answer; one wasn't forthcoming.

A slight flicker pinged the tracker I had trained on Zeke's energy. If I hadn't been paying close attention, I'd have missed it. A journey casting jumped to my call.

I hesitated.

Had I truly sensed the white wolf? Or was someone fucking with me?

I tested my connection with Zeke. It had retreated to the blockage I'd sensed. A vision of my familiar pinned to the ground by wires that had cut into his flesh rose to taunt me.

Witches had done that to him when he refused to return to the guild house with them.

I'd never known the sisterhood to harm a familiar, yet they'd done damage to mine.

Fuck it.

I had a clue. Regardless if it was real or not, I had to follow it.

Zeke was out there maybe fighting for his existence. Witches are immortal. Familiars live a long while, but their vibrant energy withers after many centuries. They don't die, but they fade away and retreat to the world that spawned them.

My spell hung before me, ripe for the plucking.

I ignited it and girded myself for damn near anything. Damien would be frantic when he returned and we were gone. Couldn't be helped. When I got back—if I got back—I'd explain everything.

The parking lot where I'd been zipping this way and that hoping for a miracle ceded to the usual darkness of a travel channel. Because my last trips had been over so quickly, I assumed this one would spit me out somewhere in short order.

Yeah. Right.

Nothing about this was normal.

The fine hairs at the back of my neck stood on end. Had I walked right into a trap?

I rocked from foot to foot, undecided. Should I abort this casting and aim for the hotel I'd just left? If I did, would it make any difference?

If you let this go, an inner voice reminded me, *you'll lose any connection with Zeke.*

Maybe not lose, but my sole clue was the whisper of a location that had stuttered past our usually bulletproof connection. Had Zeke pushed it through at great risk to himself? Or had whoever nabbed him slipped up momentarily?

Regardless, I had to see this through to its end. Or at least longer than I'd given it to bear fruit.

I've always found teleport channels soothing. Not this time, which was weird since this was my casting. Except it felt wrong, perverted, not like my magic at all.

Breathe. Just Breathe. You're mind-tripping yourself.

I took one shallow breath, aiming to fill lungs that seemed to have forgotten how to process oxygen. Maybe that was the problem. I was lightheaded because I was hyperventilating.

Another breath. And then one more.

I was breathing better, but nothing else had changed. A pervasive wrongness hung in the air around me. Rather than the clean witchy smell of spells humming along, mine had developed undernotes of rot.

If it didn't go away soon, I'd have to redirect my casting. As things stood, I grew more and more certain I was heading straight into the bowels of Hell, except not the usual one.

My trajectory wasn't leading to Satan's realm but to a far older, darker spot.

You can't know that. My inner maven was back.

I took a break from conjecture—all it did was make me

feel worse—and sent energy along my tenuous link with Zeke.

Whoa. Yes! I fist-pumped the air.

No more barrier. The wolf might be a prisoner, but I was heading straight toward him. I prepared myself to grab him —and Sita—and leave immediately.

A bit premature since I'm not exactly anywhere yet.

I told my inner voice to shut up. Half of magic is visualizing results and believing in them. It's one of the first lessons we learn when we entrain our power.

Feeling mildly guilty for not checking immediately, I pinged the tracker trained on Sita. She was in the same place as Zeke. It was good news. At least they had each other.

Nothing for this but to wait it out. I was close. This shouldn't take more than a few minutes.

Shouldn't.

Time ticked past. At least another quarter hour by my reckoning.

I reached for Zeke again. Still where I'd sensed him last time. Sita too.

Was I destined to float forever, never actually arriving?

We'll see about that.

I switched up the energy powering my travel spell, pouring fire into it. The earthy parts dropped away. My skin grew warm. Sweat beaded my forehead and dripped down my sides.

When I checked on Zeke, I was closer than I'd been before.

"Close but no cigar," I mumbled and piled still more fire into my spell stoking it with air. The channel grew unbearably hot, so hot the walls glowed red, illuminating the darkness.

My temper has always been an impediment, but anger holds its own power. Hanging onto a vision of my wolf, I shouted power words—words that should never see the light of day, or in this case a between-worlds channel—and kept them coming.

My ears hurt. My heart ached. My head was about to burst open. I didn't care, not about any of it. My objective was Zeke and Sita. I wouldn't stop until we were together.

Blood seeped beneath my fingernails and from my eyes. It had to be blood from the coppery scent. My body couldn't take much more, so I gathered everything I had into a single final push.

The channel shattered around me. I fell, cartwheeling downward until I righted myself and slowed my descent with magic. Where in the fuck was I? Had to be off world since this place didn't feel like Earth.

"Zeke!" I didn't bother with telepathy.

A robust howl filled my ears, the most welcome sound ever. Sita's caws joined the wolf's song.

I fired a mage light in time to see what looked like the bottom of a mine shaft just before I landed. Zeke and Sita rushed to me.

"Do not let go of your magic," Zeke woofed.

"Aye, you'll never get it back again," Sita cawed.

I closed my arms around Zeke. Sita nestled into my hair, talons curved around a shoulder.

"What happened?" I asked.

"Try to leave now," Zeke urged.

"Before they come back," Sita added. "Explanations can wait."

"Who?" I demanded needing to know what manner of evil we faced.

Zeke bit me gently. *"Try to leave,"* he repeated, his message urgent since he's never bitten me before.

The dregs of my altered travel spell hadn't gone anywhere. My new, improved magic didn't appear to have run down much. I gathered the edges of my tattered spell and shaped it into a more normal casting. Once I had it well in hand, I draped it around the wolf and hawk and barked another power word to kindle it.

No halfways here. Since Zeke was worried, if I didn't goose it from the gate, we'd never escape.

I waited, fully expecting the mine shaft to shimmer and vanish.

It didn't.

Of course, it didn't.

Why should this be easy when nothing else had been?

"Try harder." Zeke howled to punctuate his words. What wasn't he telling me? He's usually not frantic about anything.

Because it had magic of its own, witch magic that might help me, I visualized our stronghold in the Old Country. The spot my erstwhile sisters had held Mother after they kidnapped her. The place had been deserted for years. Maybe it still was—assuming I could get us there.

I wrapped an arm around Zeke. Touch helps with spells. Sita was already clinging to me. The hawk seemed as rattled as the wolf.

"Stay with me, no matter what," I cautioned before pounding every scrap of magic at my disposal into getting us out of this pit.

Something was coming. I had no idea what—and couldn't spare the magic to find out—but darkness bore down on us. It might have made the difference. Maybe I tried harder. All of a sudden, the mine shaft blew to smithereens. The power of my spell combined with the explosion catapulted us into another travel channel.

This one didn't feel much healthier than the last one had, but we weren't in it for long. In a staggering return to my new normal, the spell spit us out next to the postern gate of the crumbling castle where Mother had been held prisoner. It was broad daylight, but no one intercepted our arrival.

I'd blown through so much magic so quickly, my vision hazed gray. I swayed on my feet, certain I was on the verge of passing out. Zeke bit me again.

"Not yet. We are not safe. Follow me."

With the last of my consciousness and an absurd amount of effort, I trudged carefully placing one foot ahead of the other as my wolf, my protector, my darling, led us to the mouth of a cave, through a tunnel, and then into its cool, murky depths.

I trusted him. He understood how depleted I was.

We stopped next to an underground pool with sandy banks. I sank first to a crouch and then lay on one side breathing as if I'd just run a marathon. The hawk traded my shoulder for the ground next to me.

"What happened?" I rasped. "Who nearly had us?"

"Naught you can do about it now," Sita cawed. "We will keep watch."

Zeke stretched full length against me. I dropped an arm around him, still not believing we were together again. A confused jumble of questions and relief bounced from one side of my mind to the other. Somewhere in between, a chiaroscuro curtain muffled my disquiet, and I passed out.

CHAPTER TWELVE,
DAMIEN

Following Morgan's energy, and fully warded, I made my way cautiously around twists and turns in an extensive underground tunnel system. Before I got far, the distinctive stench of Banshees hit me in the solar plexus.

What were they doing here?

I've never known one to leave the Highlands.

I slowed still more, testing the air for clues. Banshees, for sure, but also a Kelpie. Neither could have traveled here on their own. Outraged whinnies and shrieks only a Banshee can produce made my ears ache. Though I stretched my senses, I didn't hear Zeke's signature howl or the hawk's cries.

Hoping to hell my invisibility casting was as bombproof as I needed it to be, I hustled to the next bend in the tunnel system. It opened to a cavern that might have belonged to an abandoned mine.

Morgan's energy was all over the place, but she was gone.

Hot damn! She'd escaped and taken her familiars along for the ride. I'd have hooted with glee except it would have alerted the odd collection of escapees from the Highlands about my existence.

I melted into a declination in a nearby wall and waited. Someone was running this show. I had to know who and settled in to wait. Now that I knew Morgan was safe, I could spare a few minutes.

"Quit your caterwauling," a harsh voice shouted.

Ha! Didn't have to wait long after all.

A tall regal man strode through a wall and into the mix. His chest was bare, and a pair of leather breeks was slung low on his hips. Flaxen hair cascaded to waist level; ice-blue eyes glared disapprovingly. A squared off chin and high forehead lent him a patrician air.

Silence descended on the pit.

The Banshees dropped to the ground. The Kelpie just stared at him and stamped a hoof. "Give it a break, Hermes. You don't own us."

I tightened my spell.

Hermes, huh? Crap. I'd expected witches or demons, not a Greek god. I'd crossed paths with a few over the years, but never him.

"How did you lose them?" he thundered. "We set the perfect trap."

"Not perfect enough, apparently." A woman oozed through the same wall. About the same height as Hermes, she wore a simple white gown that ended at her knees. Old-fashioned lace-up buff leather boots covered her feet and calves. A copper torc circled her neck. Dark hair fell to shoulder level; silver eyes scanned the cavern. Her nostrils twitched.

"She was here," the woman noted.

"Don't belabor the obvious, Hera," Hermes snapped.

Fuck me. Another big gun. The Greeks were just as set against Hecate getting her hands on Morgan now as they'd been hundreds of years ago. A piece of news worth filing away. Maeve had warned me, but I'd discounted her fears.

"We'll figure something else out," the Kelpie neighed.

"Like what?" Hermes eyed the Scottish water horse.

"Not sure. Something. Get us out of this hellhole. I told you it was too far away to be useful."

The Banshees were still prostrate. None of them had so much as flicked an ear.

"How dare you correct my decisions." Hera stood tall and glared at the horse. A thread of glittering magic arced from her to the Kelpie.

He didn't so much as flinch.

"I'll do as I please. Get yourself another patsy. This game grows stale." The horse shook his coal black mane.

Hermes angled a pointed look at the horse. "Fine. Get back on your own."

The Kelpie's next move was lightning fast—and so unexpected—I nearly forgot about holding onto my invisibility casting. He lunged at Hermes and sank his squared-off equine teeth into the god's upper arm.

Blood welled around the wound.

"You forget your place," Hera shrilled and fired another far denser salvo of power at the horse.

He didn't let go.

Because he couldn't talk and bite at the same time, guttural mind speech filled the cavern. *I will release him once you give your word you will return us—all of us—to our home in the Highlands.*

Hermes appeared to be working power on his end. His body took on a glowing aspect, except it included the Kelpie. Clearly, any teleport spell would encompass the horse.

"This was your brilliant idea. Fix it." Hera shook a fist at Hermes and vanished.

He stared after her gape-mouthed, as if he couldn't believe she'd deserted him. A moment passed, and then one more. His blood dripped on the cavern floor.

"You have my word," he gritted.

"About?" the Kelpie inquired sweetly.

"I will return all of you to the Highlands as soon as you release me."

"No tricks," the horse warned bluntly.

"No tricks."

The Kelpie opened his massive jaws and pranced to one side. One by one, the Banshees sprang upright surrounding the horse. They were making it simple for Hermes to forge a group casting.

Rather than tending to his wound, which was bleeding profusely, the god spoke a few words, waved his hands, and the motley crew disappeared.

"Fuck." Hermes sank to a crouch. His injured arm took on an eldritch glow as he worked on healing it.

I could have left, probably should have, but we were alone. Last I checked, there wasn't any particular animosity between the Fae and the Greek gods. In a bold move I hoped I didn't regret, I shucked my warding and strode forward.

Shock reflected in Hermes' widened eyes and raised brows.

I stuck out a hand. "I'm Damien, one of the elder Fae. I don't believe we've met formally."

"No shit. Never seen you before, ever." Hermes pushed upright, ignoring my extended hand. "What in the fuck are you doing here, Fae?"

A truth net clanked into place encompassing me. Rude of him. Usually, we save the Draconian measures for when they're truly needed.

"I was tracking Morgan, a witch and my soon-to-be mate."

The truth net clanked a warning at the soon-to-be mate part.

Hermes huffed out a breath and spun one hand in a get-on-with it motion.

"She hasn't exactly agreed to the mating part, but we're moving in that direction," I clarified. It satisfied the truth net, which pinged cleanly.

"Are you working alone? Or do you carry blessings from the rest of your kin?"

How to answer that one?

"The Fae know what I'm doing. No one has tried to stop

me. Our seer did warn me the Greeks who imprisoned Hecate might not take kindly to me assisting Morgan."

A perfectly toned chime verified my words. I batted at the weave. "Could we dispense with this? It's demeaning."

The net clattered to the floor.

Hermes rounded on me and thumped my chest with his index finger. "Stay out of our business. You know nothing about our affairs."

I started to correct him, say I knew more than he imagined, but wisely kept my mouth shut. Instead, I asked, "Why would it be so dangerous to allow Hecate access to her creation? Witches are falling to darkness at an alarming rate. If someone doesn't step in, there may be no white witches left."

"Not our problem. Not Hecate's, either, until she hatched that absurd scheme to reinvent herself as savior to all witches." He sneered. "I blame Circe and Medea."

"Where are they these days?" May as well gather what information I could.

"We have no idea," he sneered. "They made themselves scarce after we imprisoned Hecate."

"I'm still not seeing why Hecate accessing Morgan is so bad."

Another chest thump. "You don't have to see a damned thing, Fae. You have been warned. Keep away from Hecate. Do not aid nor abet her."

"She's free," I pointed out.

"You think we don't know as much," he thundered.

"Probably won't be so simple to snare her a second time, huh?"

"If you must know, we're working on it now." False assurance laced into his words.

For all his hubris, I must have stumbled onto a sore spot. He swung at me, fist connecting to my jaw. If I'd been built like a normal Fae, I'd have hit the ground. He hadn't counted on my beefy build or on me fighting back.

One benefit of my long years working construction was a passing familiarity with barroom brawls.

I hit him squarely on the side of his neck. He staggered back a step, an incredulous expression spreading over his face. My bet was no one had ever punched him before.

Both my hands were fisted, feinting and hunting for a target. If he wanted it up close and personal, I'd give it to him. Adrenaline flowing, I welcomed a good scrap particularly with someone as arrogant as one of the Greeks.

He fell back a step, glaring and rubbing his neck.

"What's the matter?" I taunted. "You can dish it out, but you can't take it?" Not the smartest move, but in for a penny in for a pound.

His chiseled mouth split into a grin. "This is bad, but I like you."

Color me shocked. I dropped my fists to my sides, eying him warily. "If you like me so much, stop hounding Morgan. She has enough problems with the sorceress witches who kicked her out of her Coven. They've never quit harassing her."

"Not my bailiwick. Leave now, Fae, before I change my mind."

His words were hollow. Both of us knew as much. He couldn't have held me there if he tried. I grabbed the moral high ground, allowed him to cling to false dignity, and set a teleport spell back to the bed and breakfast. Surely, Morgan and the animals would have returned there to wait for me.

Except they hadn't.

The room was just as empty as it had been when I left it. No one had returned in betwixt and between. Hours had passed; it was nearly checkout time. Should I extend our reservation for one more day and wait? It seemed like money well spent, particularly since Morgan's things were still here, so I visited the front desk.

That done, I returned to the room.

It would be available should Morgan return. I considered waiting, but it didn't set well. I should look for her, but where? If I tracked her from here, I'd end up right back where I'd just left.

A small notepad sat on the bureau along with a pen. I scratched out a note.

If you return, stay put, please.

It looked a shred on the stark side, so I tacked *Love, Damien* onto the end.

I dropped my phone, still sitting next to the bed, into a pocket and went outside. Maybe if I walked around a bit an idea would jar itself loose. As I covered distance, I replayed my conversation with Hermes. I should have asked about his connection with the Banshees and Kelpie. Their presence made me wonder if the Greeks hadn't thrown in their lot with Coven witches.

It made sense since both contingents were dead set against Morgan and Hecate joining forces. Circumstances make for strange bedfellows.

Banshees.

They're actually a type of Faery. As such, they're subservient to us. It wasn't a guarantee they'd talk with me, but I had a starting place. All I had to do was find them. Hundreds of years ago, it was a simpler prospect.

Because it was a likely spot, I returned to the graveyard with its collection of falling in crypts. Banshees like dark places. Light doesn't damage them like it does vampires, but they avoid it because their appearance terrifies mortals who hasten to summon emergency services.

Paranormal detective agencies are ubiquitous. Organizations similar to the one that had kidnapped me are on this side of the Atlantic too. When they locate supernaturals, they grasp any excuse to imprison us.

Beginning on one side of the old section of the graveyard, I visited crypts until I found what I was certain had to be there: the entrance to a vast underground tunnel system. The characteristic stench of Banshees, part rot and part flowers, led me straight to one of their lairs.

I pulled a decrepit gate aside and strode within. "Look sharp." I snapped my fingers.

A dozen Banshees raced toward me—and stopped dead.

"Fae," one gasped.

"What are you doing here?" another demanded.

"I have questions. You will answer them." Better to lead out strong with underlings.

"What's in it for us?" a third simpered.

"I won't report your lair to the PDA."

A cacophony of boos and hisses filled the air. I shrugged.

"Take it or leave it. Are you working with witches or any of the Greek gods to stymie Hecate?"

They glared at me, mulish expressions on their misshapen faces. Banshees are always female. Once, they may have been attractive, but something about the transition from human to Banshee obliterated any trace of beauty.

"I'm counting to ten," I told the group. "If no one says anything by the time I hit ten, I'm leaving. And you'd best scuttle to relocate. One, two, three…"

I hit nine before a scrawny woman with patchy blonde hair stepped forward. "Aye, we're working with them. What's it to you?"

"What did they promise you?"

"Nothing."

"Then why'd you agree to help?" I asked.

A shrug. "Naught better to do."

"So, are the Greeks and witches in cahoots?"

The Banshee hesitated so long, I turned to leave. Spectral hands clawed at my sleeve. I turned, breathing shallowly to avoid a lungful of her stench. "I don't have all day."

She nodded. "Best we can tell. We're at the bottom of the food chain. No one tells us much of anything."

"And the Kelpies too?"

She made a face and spat in the dirt. "They're witchy tools. That's old news."

I felt certain the Kelpies didn't view themselves as anyone's tool, but it explained why the one off-world had told Hermes to pound sand.

"Thanks." I headed for the entrance.

"That's all?" one called after me.

I didn't bother answering. They'd given me what I needed. Escaping from the fetid tunnel into fresh air was welcome. Time to return to the bed and breakfast. The room was still empty.

Where in the hell had she and the animals gone? It was a longshot, but I raised my mind voice. Of course, she didn't answer.

Only one avenue left to me. I'd return to the borderworld where I'd last sensed her and track her from there. It might work unless she'd taken care to conceal her destination.

Too tense to sit, I paced from one side of the room to the other and back again. How had the witches garnered cooperation from the Greeks? Surely, if the gods understood the full extent of the witches' foray into dark power, they'd never have joined forces with them.

Maybe.

I'd told Hermes flat out about corrupt witches; he hadn't cared. Breath whistled from between my teeth. Talk about a marriage of convenience. Did no one have principles anymore?

Determined to find Morgan, I gathered my flagging magic into yet one more spell. I'd need food soon, but if I were careful, I could eke what I needed out of what remained in my reservoir.

I hated to divert any magic, but I fashioned a primitive ward and held it at the ready. No reason to deploy it if the mineshaft—or whatever it was—turned out to be empty.

My stay-put note was still on the dresser. It was the best I could do.

Tossing a prayer to Danu ahead of my spell, I drew a portal and stepped through. Next stop was the borderworld. If I'd been smarter, I'd have tracked Morgan the first time, except it never occurred to me she'd do anything but return here.

CHAPTER THIRTEEN, MORGAN

Zeke was still lying next to me when my eyes fluttered open. The cave didn't offer any clues about how much time had passed, but I felt considerably better than when I'd passed out.

The wolf licked my neck. I hugged him before rolling to a sit.

"Okay, tell me what happened. How'd the two of you end up off-world?"

"We're not entirely certain," Sita cawed.

"One minute, we were asleep," Zeke chimed in. *"The next we were caught up in a travel channel."*

"Was there any warning?" Worry clawed at me. I vowed to never let either familiar out of my sight ever again.

"If there had been, we'd have fought back," Zeke woofed.

"Or made a bunch of noise to alert you," the hawk squawked. She flew to my shoulder; I stroked her feathers.

"Of course you would have," I murmured. "What happened next?"

"They dropped us in that cave. The transport went fast."

"We never actually saw who was behind everything," Sita clarified.

"Their scent was...odd," Zeke confirmed. *"We tried to find a way out, but then a horde of Banshees showed up along with one Kelpie."*

Crap. My sister witches were at it again, except this time they'd nabbed my familiars since they'd already killed my mother.

"What did they do?" I asked, proud my voice didn't quiver. I wasn't frightened, but fury beat a track through me. Maybe it had been a mistake not to tackle vengeance against the Coven first. Hecate had waited this long; she could wait a few more weeks or months.

"They didn't smell right," Zeke woofed. *"So I asked who'd given orders to capture us."*

"They laughed at us. Laughed." Sita squawked with outrage.

"And then all the Banshees' heads swiveled in the same direction. The Kelpie scraped a hoof in the dirt."

"It was like they all heard something we didn't," Sita chirped.

"Must have because they ran through an opening and disappeared," Zeke woofed.

"And then you showed up," Sita burrowed deeper into my shoulder. "They knew you were there and were on their way back. It was why Zeke urged you to hurry."

So that was what I'd felt. If I hadn't been under so much

pressure, I'd have diverted enough power to figure it out on my own.

"Was it hard finding us?" Zeke woofed.

"More difficult than I'd have liked. Our link was perverted. Some kind of barrier worked against me. It was harder than hell to break through."

"Doesn't make sense," the hawk chirped.

"Why not?" I asked her. "Maybe they wanted my power as depleted as possible to make it simpler to snare me."

"Never thought of that," the hawk admitted.

"We assumed it was you they wanted," Zeke added. *"And that you'd be along immediately. I tried reaching through our link to warn you, but something kept getting in the way."*

I scratched his ears. "Yeah, the same something stood between me and your location. It was like someone was doling out data on a need-to-know basis."

"None of it matters." Zeke rubbed his head against me. *"We're together again."*

I clapped a hand over my mouth. We were missing a critical element. Damien. He had to be worried sick about us. Would he be at the bed and breakfast? Or was he out combing the countryside using his Fae tracking ability?

"What?" Zeke got his feet under him and shook himself from head to tail tip.

"We have to get back. Damien has no idea where we are." Crap. Even though I'd decided against it at the time, I should have left some kind of note, even one written in obscure terms.

Footsteps sounded in the tunnel leading to our hiding place.

Damn it. Was fighting my way out of jams the new normal? At least my magic was back online.

Zeke's ears pricked forward. Tail pluming, he raced toward whoever was coming. I couldn't let my wolf face danger alone, so I sprinted after him. The forest smells of Fae reached me. My heart battered against my ribcage. I had to get hold of myself. I was way too over-the-top happy Damien had found us.

A happy woof and Damien's rich, deep laughter told me Zeke had reached him.

Sita launched off my shoulder, winging her way down the center of the tunnel.

When I joined them, Zeke had his paws on Damien's shoulders, and Sita sat on his head cooing like a mourning dove.

"You're a hard woman to find," Damien said as he patted Zeke, grabbed his front paws, and placed them on the ground.

He always elicits the same reaction from me. He's so larger than life he absorbs all the oxygen. My chest felt tight. Anticipation narrowed my throat. I fought an inane urge to throw myself into his arms and never let go.

"Sorry," I mumbled. "Thought about leaving a note, but at the time I didn't know who'd kidnapped Zeke and Sita. Anything I wrote could have given my position away."

Fair brows shot up. "They didn't take all of you together?"

I bristled. "Do you think I would have let that happen?"

"I don't get it. You were together."

Guilt warmed my cheeks. "I went into the bathroom to

take a quick shower. When I came out, the room was empty."

"Hmmm. I see."

I dug my teeth into my lower lip. Just how much did he see? Had he spent enough time in the room to catch a whiff of my arousal? Had he sensed my slight bending of the truth? I didn't want to lie to him, but neither was I about to tell him I'd been so smitten by lust I'd taken a private moment.

"It's really good to see you," I ventured to move the subject off why I hadn't kept a closer eye on Zeke and Sita.

"Goes double for me, wench. I've been hunting you for hours. Made two trips to that infernal mineshaft." He winced. "Mostly because I wasn't smart enough to track you the first time I left. I assumed you'd return to the hotel."

I turned my hands palms up. "I already apologized. We need a better method of communicating."

"We have one," he reminded me. "The crystal Maeve gave you."

Oops. Fuck.

"Damn. I forgot about it. This isn't exactly an excuse, but I was so frantic when I discovered the animals were gone, the last thing on my mind was that stone. Besides, I'm pretty sure I left it in the closet."

"You did. I extended our stay another day, so presumably it's still there."

Feeling embarrassed as sin at my lapse, I placed a hand on his arm. "I'm not used to checking in. With anyone. But I won't forget about the crystals a second time. Promise."

He shook his head. "You've been through hell, and here I

am grilling you. Apologies. It's just I've been so worried—or I was until I hit the mineshaft, knew you'd been there and made good on your escape. Strong work."

"We'd have come back to the hotel, but I was sucking fumes, so I took us to the old witch stronghold. You know it. You've been here."

"Why was that simpler?"

I offered half a smile. "Same reason Faery is the easiest spot for you to teleport to. Magic calls to its own. I wasn't making any progress getting out of there until I switched destinations."

"I should have thought of that."

He placed a hand over mine and then drew me into an embrace. I leaned into him, breathing him in and wishing we could stop time. I was sick of renegade witches, imperious gods, and the shithole my life had turned into ever since the Coven kicked me to the curb.

Give it a rest. A pity party won't help.

"I want to hunt," Zeke informed me.

"Me too," Sita said.

I tilted my head back. "What do you think? There's far more game here than in Carlisle, but I'm not sure I trust them unescorted."

"How about this? We'll all go outside. Once they've caught dinner, we'll wait while they eat. Then we'll go back to the bed and breakfast."

Zeke must have approved because he took off at a lope for the tunnel opening a short distance ahead. Sita followed.

Damien and I hurried after them and settled in an evergreen grove to keep a watchful eye on things. The wolf and hawk stuck close. They didn't want a repeat of earlier, either.

"While I was in the mineshaft, I had a run in with Hermes," Damien said. "Hera too, but she left quickly. And she didn't know I was there."

I'd been crouched in the dirt, leaning against him. His words tumbled me onto my ass. "As in the Greeks?"

"The same. Maeve was right. They don't want Hecate anywhere near you. I didn't ask enough questions, but Hermes might not have answered even if I did. So I ran down a few Banshees once I was back in Scotland. They corroborated my suspicion."

"Which is?"

"Exigency makes for strange partnerships. The Greeks don't give a damn witches are falling into sorcerous ways. They've partnered with them to ensure you and Hecate never get together. It's how Banshees and a Kelpie ended up in the mineshaft."

"I never saw them," I muttered.

"We did. Already told you," Zeke informed me from his spot devouring a pile of rodent carcasses.

"Good they didn't bother you," Damien murmured.

"Not for lack of effort. I felt darkness bearing down on me as I was trying to get out of there."

Sita worked her way through three mice. Zeke demolished a pile of assorted dinner items. It was nearing dusk when they finished. I'd been wary and watchful, but hadn't sensed anything unusual.

"Ready to go back?" Damien pushed to his feet.

I did the same. "Yes. Our turn for dinner."

Damien laced his fingers with mine, chanted low, and draped a spell over us all. When it cleared, we were back in our room. Someone had tidied up. Zeke tilted his snout, sniffing.

"Has anyone been here besides a housekeeper?" I asked.

"I don't think so. No witches." He curled up in his spot beneath the window.

Sita perched on a dresser and tucked her head beneath a wing.

"I'm going to clean up." Damien ambled into the bathroom.

I hunted around for a menu. No kitchen here, but many services like Door Dash offered to bring the selection of your choice to your hotel. After checking with Damien through the door, I ordered an oversized charcuterie board with a decent wine and extra bread.

By the time he emerged from the shower, fragrant and with his long hair rippling around his shoulders, our food had arrived. He hadn't bothered to put his clothing back on. Instead, a robe provided by the hotel was draped around his shoulders and sashed at his waist. The visual was far more enticing than our supper, but we needed food more than extracurricular pursuits. Besides, we lacked privacy.

We ate in a companionable silence until I asked, "So, what's next?"

Surprise radiated from him; he set his wine down. "What do you mean? We haven't located Hecate."

"Is it worth pissing off every witch and Banshee and Kelpie, never mind the Greek gods?" I blew out a breath. "I'm tired."

"Tired enough to sit back while witchdom is absorbed by darkness?"

Ouch. "You don't play fair."

He reached across the small table. I grasped his hand. "We've come too far to throw in our cards," he said.

"If Hecate was still interested, don't you think she'd have gotten hold of me somehow? If she's given up, who are we to press the issue?"

On his feet in a trice, he crossed to my side of the table and scooped me into his arms. "That doesn't sound like the witch I fell in love with."

"Being chased and hounded and never having a moment's peace does that to a person." My words were muffled against his chest.

He twined fingers into my hair. "You're Fate's child, Morgan. Have been ever since you made the decision to shelve your glamour."

I tilted my head back and did a deep dive into his green eyes. "Does it mean I can't ever get off the merry-go-round?

"Do you really want to?"

His words were soft; they arrowed straight into my soul. Before I could answer, he angled his head and closed his mouth over mine. He tasted of the oaky chardonnay that had come with our dinner. I didn't mean to, but I tossed my arms around his broad back, rose on tiptoes, and crushed my mouth into his kiss.

Done with denying the attraction that had smoldered between us from the very first day, I pressed my tongue into his mouth and sparred with his when he did the same. He kneaded my shoulders before running his fingertips down my back until his hands cupped the globes of my ass, drawing me against his fully erect cock.

He trailed kisses across my cheek and down my neck to the hollow in my collarbone. I teased his ear with my tongue, running it along the delicate pointed tip. My thighs slicked with moisture; my nipples pebbled with need. He rocked against me, the length of him pressed into my stomach.

I've never touched a man. The draw of that hot, hard appendage was compelling, so much so I snaked a hand between us and cradled him. Damien moaned and dug his fingers deeper into my ass cheeks.

The harsh rasp of our breath filled the room.

Every point of contact turned electric. The air took on a numinous glow as magic spilled from us. I've never wanted anything as badly as I craved Damien.

Except we weren't alone.

He tossed an arm under my legs and gathered me into his arms as he walked us toward the bed, still kissing me. Once he laid me on the comforter, he turned out the lights with a shot of magic. I rolled over so I could pull the covers out of the way, but stopped when I remembered how dirty my clothes were.

Damien chanted softly, fingers weaving in a pattern that created a kaleidoscopic array of color that surrounded the bed. I could see through it, but I had a feeling it was opaque from the other side.

He was creating the privacy he'd sensed I needed. As his spell circled the bed, he shucked the robe from his shoulders. I'd begun to unlace my boots, but I stopped and stared gape mouthed.

The reality of Damien was so much more intense than any of my imaginings, I had trouble absorbing his beauty. Shoulders slabbed with muscle gave way to golden nipples, a flat stomach, and slender hips. When I remembered to breathe, my gaze sought the proud column of flesh rising from a spiky mat of fair curls. His legs were spectacular: long, lean, and worthy of one of the gods.

He knelt before me and levered off my boots and stockings. Next, he undid the zipper and button holding my pants in place, coaxing them down my legs. The musk of my arousal surrounded us. His nostrils twitched as he inhaled my scent.

A quick check reassured me Zeke and Sita were still asleep. Damien had crafted the impossible, a one-way sound-and-sight shield where we could ensure nothing harmed them.

"It's not perfect," he murmured, "but it will do."

"You're perfect." I wriggled while he tugged my top over my head. My sports bra followed. I've never been naked in front of a man. Would he find me pleasing?

Suddenly shy, I crossed my arms in front of my breasts.

He pried them away. "It's a crime against nature to cover such perfection."

"I've never—" I began not sure where to go from there. My cheeks, already warm from lust, heated still further.

Reaching past me, he finished turning down the bed. Arms around me, he guided us until our heads were on the pillows. Old-fashioned down, they were fragrant with lavender. I reached behind me to deal with a lump and came up with a heart-shaped Dove chocolate.

The housekeeper must have left it. After unwrapping the foil, I bit it in half and fed part to Damien.

When he gathered me in his arms and kissed me, we both tasted of chocolate, sweet and piquant. I'd been worried lovemaking would be awkward, but Damien's embrace was the most natural thing in the world.

I scattered a couple of beacons near Zeke and Sita to warn me if anything disturbed their peace.

"I should have done that," he murmured.

"You crafted privacy." I nuzzled his neck. "We make a good team."

"I've been telling you that from the first day we met."

"You're sounding suspiciously like a know-it-all, but I still love you."

"Say it again," he demanded.

"I love you." As the words spilled from me, the truth in them swatted me between the eyes.

"Good because I love you."

Kisses took the place of words.

Doubts fled, and for once I stopped thinking. The only thing in the world was Damien's body pressed against mine, his lips roving my flesh, and the silk of his skin beneath my fingers.

CHAPTER FOURTEEN, DAMIEN

Morgan's body exceeded every fantasy I'd spun. High, full breasts with generous coppery nipples, shapely shoulders, a rounded belly, and a to-die-for ass. Men would fight wars over that ass even if it weren't paired with gorgeous dancer's legs and feet with high arches.

I ran my nails up the soles of her feet when I took off her boots, loving how she pressed them into my hands. I'd done the best I could to accomplish two goals: relative privacy for the lovemaking I hoped would follow and the ability to keep an eye on Zeke and Sita.

Like most magical constructs, my barrier had flaws, but it would do for our purposes.

Between sharing chocolate and kisses, she told me she loved me. It rocked my world to the core. So much so, I asked to hear it again. For whatever reason, her ambivalence had shifted. Immortals rarely fall in love. The odds of maintaining a relationship over eons aren't good. Far better to engage in a series of less-committed adventures.

Except it wasn't what I wanted. Not with Morgan.

Nope. I wanted her next to me through all the long years of our lives. I'd have told her, but I didn't want to scare her away.

Kisses were familiar territory, but I ached to explore all of her, worship her with my tongue and fingers. I licked my way down her neck, around a collarbone to a pebbled nipple. When I took it into my mouth, she arched her back, pushing into me.

She kneaded my shoulders, running her nails down my back as far as she could reach. Nothing tentative about her touch. Filling my hands with her breasts, I lashed my tongue from one to the other, biting and suckling. One of my legs was between hers; she writhed against my thigh.

Reaching between us, she captured the length of me in a hand. Her touch was intense, incredible as she explored my shaft. All this was new to her. In a rush of sexist delight mingled with feral protectiveness, I was ecstatic to be her first lover.

She teased my cock with gentle strokes followed by firm ones. I yearned for the heat of her vault around me, but she wasn't ready yet. I disentangled her hand and moved lower.

"Did I do something wrong?"

"Not at all, darling. Not at all."

I hovered over the mat of dark curls at the entrance to her sex, inhaling the delicious musk of her. Witch spice raised to the ninth power. Bending, I swirled my tongue around her glistening pearl. Her hips bucked, and she cried out, so I did it once more before fastening my mouth over the center of her sensation.

Two fingers slipped inside the intense heat and slickness of her body. Muscles contracted around them, but I took things slow. Tongue swirls, breathing, suckling guided her over the edge. As she came, I circled the fingers inside her, widening her passage. Her back arched. Spasms rippled through her accompanied by mewls of delight.

Despite my aching shaft and my triple-time breathing, I planned to do this at least once more.

She dragged at the sides of my head. "I want you inside me."

"Do you now?" The taste of her was thick on my lips. It increased my arousal still more.

"We can play twenty questions later. We've come this far. Fuck me." Her hands were on my shoulders, tugging me upward.

What can I say? Men are weak, and I'd dreamed of loving Morgan since I first laid eyes on her.

I knelt between her thighs nesting the head of my cock in the soft folds of her. Edging forward, I angled toward her opening. She spread her legs and wrapped them around my waist. Both of us were panting, chests heaving. Her breasts were splotched a lovely rose color also painting her chest and cheeks.

A quick glance at Zeke and Sita reassured me they were still here and still asleep. Or pretending to be. Who knew just how effective my barrier was?

I stopped thinking of anything other than the tip of me buried at the entrance to her sex. Determined to take this slow, I inched inside. She didn't make it easy with her hips bucking and rocking and hands on my hips tugging me forward. Covering her breasts with my hands, I rubbed her nipples.

Her muscles contracted around me, drawing me farther inside. I moved in tiny increments, not wanting to hurt her, but her vault swelled around me absorbing my length and girth.

Finally, we were fully joined. My breath came in panting gasps. My errant member was harder than hard.

Ever so slowly, I began to withdraw. She waited until I was almost all the way out to jackknife her body under mine and roll me onto my back where she straddled me, sinking onto my shaft.

Her expression contorted as waves of delight coursed through both of us. "This is better," she rasped, moving her hips in a circular motion. To balance herself, she splayed her hands on my chest pinching my nipples before she settled her mouth atop mine.

I grasped her hips and drove into her. It was what she wanted. Orgasms ripped through her. After two more, I couldn't hold back. Semen boiled from my balls in long, lazy gouts. Ecstasy is its own dance. Once I gave into its pull, I came for a long time.

We lay in one another's arms as our breathing stabilized. I twitched my member still sunk deep in her body and shifted us onto our sides.

She twitched back. "That was incredible. I had no idea what I've been missing."

"It was amazing." I licked her neck and ear. "Because you're amazing."

She bolted from my embrace, gaze seeking her familiars. Relief poured off her in waves. "I didn't exactly forget about them—" she began.

I placed a hand over her mouth. "Ssht. I get it. I checked on them too."

"The beacons would have alerted me, but witches can disable them." Morgan relaxed into my embrace. "We should savor this. Who knows when we'll get another moment together."

I winced.

"What?" Her lush lips curved in a soft smile.

"I'd like nothing more than to whisk us all to Faery, but we can't do that."

"We could, but I'd always wonder what cards I left on the table."

"Me too." I twined fingers through her silky hair, brushing strands away from her face.

"Do you still think we should start at Lagina?"

All I wished for was more of what we'd shared, but her question jolted me back to reality. "Do you have a better idea?"

Her forehead crinkled in thought. "I keep catching bits and pieces of an island, except I have no idea where it is."

"Show me." I opened my mind to her. Images cascaded into it. Something familiar nagged, so I studied them closely. Suddenly a few neurons connected. "It could be Ikaria or Samos."

"Where are they?"

"Two small islands off the western coast of Turkey. They're the southernmost elements in the Aegean Island chain."

"Huh. Never heard of either. Are they busy?"

I nodded. "Very. Big tourist destinations."

"Not sounding like somewhere we'd find Hecate." She closed her teeth over her lower lip. "Wonder why I'm seeing them."

"Maybe Hecate planted the vision."

"Pfft. Or some other witch anxious to throw me off the scent track."

"Anything is possible," I agreed. "Let's rest for a bit, and then we'll pick which place to start."

She snugged her muscles around me. "We can rest anytime."

"Hussy."

"Don't you know it." She planted her lips on mine. Desire, sweet, thick, heady rolled through every cell. I returned her kiss with fervor, my need as sharp as if we hadn't spent the last hour pleasuring one another.

"Stop thinking," she managed around our kiss.

I didn't answer, just deepened our kiss and captured a breast. She was right. Everything beyond this moment could take a backseat. For now, brand new lovers that we were, we shut out everything but the joy we could wring from each other's bodies.

∼

AFTER HOURS OF ENDLESS INVENTIVENESS, we dozed. When I opened my eyes, light seeped from beneath the room-darkening shades. Zeke had his paws on the table polishing off the last of the cheese and cold cuts from the charcuterie board. Sita was picking off the nuts and olives.

Probably both of them needed to go outside.

Trying not to wake Morgan, I dismantled my barrier spell—it had wound down anyway without me to siphon power into it—and swung my legs over the side of the bed.

"Not so fast." Morgan snaked out a hand and grabbed my wrist.

I tousled her hair. "Time to get up, sleepyhead."

"But I want to stay here forever."

Her words lit a fire in my soul. I placed a hand over hers. "I'd love to stay in this bed for days, weeks, years, but remaining in one spot for too long isn't wise. Not with all the enemies we've collected."

Her lips were swollen from our hours of lovemaking. I ached to kiss her, but if I did, we'd end up right back in bed. I started pulling clothes on.

"I'll take Zeke out. Sita can use the window, but I'll keep an eye on her outside."

The wolf woofed softly, tail pluming. Sita did her mourning dove imitation.

Morgan nodded. "I'll take a quick shower. Be ready to leave once you get back."

I grinned. "Let's at least scare up some coffee and breakfast on our way out of town."

She glanced at the empty plate on the table and then at Zeke and arched her brows. "You helped yourself? Again?"

He yipped happily.

A snort blew past Morgan's lips. "You're hopeless."

"Nope. Hungry."

I bent to put on my socks and lace my boots. Then I picked up my discarded robe and tossed it over a chair. "Remind me what you were," I told Zeke so I could resurrect his glamour.

"This." He turned into an Australian shepherd in the blink of an eye.

Okay, then. No need for Morgan or me to manage his glamour. I cracked a window for Sita and opened the door.

"Back soon," I told Morgan and tugged it shut behind me.

Judging from the angle of the sun, it was around ten. Carlisle's streets were full of people heading this way and that. I fashioned the illusion of a leash and looped it over Zeke's head. A few folk smiled and waved. I did the same, remembering to shore up my own glamour. My hair is long enough to conceal the points of my ears, but anyone looking closely would notice them.

Eh, they'd probably assume I was into some kind of cosplay gig. Over the years, I've dropped in on science fiction and fantasy conventions. The costumes are incredible. Once I sat next to an entire family of Klingons. Their attire must have set them back ten grand.

Zeke did his doggy thing, sniffing and lifting his leg from time to time. Sita flew overhead. Hard to say who was keeping an eye on whom. I stopped at a street vendor's kiosk and bought two cups of coffee and an assortment of pastries, some sweet, others savory.

"Ready to head back, boy?" I asked Zeke.

In answer, he tugged at the leash, heading for something down a side street. I followed. "Okay, but your mother's going to be annoyed if her coffee gets cold."

"She won't mind," the wolf informed me, still intent on half dragging me down a block that had turned from retail to residential.

"Where are we going?" I asked. Hanging onto the cardboard coffee carrier, my bakery bag, and the leash was turning into a juggling act.

"I want to know too," Sita spoke up.

Zeke led me between two crumbling stone buildings. Behind them sat what looked like a shepherd's hut from England's northern moors, except this one had been transported into the city. Closer inspection revealed it was illusion, not real at all.

Suddenly cautious, I reached out a few tentative strands of seeking magic and took a step back. Whoever was in the ticky-tacky hut was oozing power. I tightened up my spell, making it smaller and more pointed.

Son of a bitch. What was a dark Fae doing here? They had their own sector of Faery. We left them alone; the feeling was mutual. No love lost between the two branches of Faery.

While I was deciding what to do next, the cabin's door creaked inward. Sita landed on my shoulder, beak clacking. Zeke growled low, hackles raising along his back as he shucked his glamour.

Cold prickling surrounded us as something blocked out the morning's light.

"Stop that," I commanded.

A hag lurched through the door stinking of spirits. I could smell her from ten paces away. For the most part, none of us over-imbibe. Dressed in a tattered black robe that hung open in front, she'd apparently given up on the spells that maintain our appearance. Her face was deeply lined, her dark eyes rheumy. Veins marked the backs of her hands and her neck. Matted white hair fell in dreads down her back.

"I'll do as I please, Fae." She slurred her words and made Fae sound like a curse.

Fine. Why had Zeke dragged us here? What instinct told him we needed to know about this particular sorceress.

"You," she squealed. "I saw you, and now here you are."

Great, not only was she booze-happy, she was also a few cards shy of a full deck. It happens with immortals, but most of us who lose it have the decency to wait out eternity in the *Dreaming*.

Pointing a crooked index finger at me, she dropped into a singsong voice. "You must not go. Bad things will happen. Return to Faery ere 'tis too late."

"Must not go where?"

"You know. Don't pretend to be thickheaded."

The spot where she'd stood was empty. The hut door thudded shut. The casting that had stood between us and the burgeoning day dropped away. I stared at the cottage, half expecting it to vanish too. It didn't, but I suspected I was the only one who could see it. Mortals probably either saw something else—or nothing at all.

"Why'd you bring us here?" I asked Zeke.

"Something pulled me in this direction. It was so strong, it had to be important."

Past time to return to Morgan. She'd be worried about us by now.

After refashioning Zeke's leash illusion, I set a brisk pace. Sita flew above us. When we got near the building, she circled around heading for the window. Foul enchantment drew my attention to a nearby copse of shrubs.

When I bent to look, a blast of power nearly blinded me. Fuck. Hex bags. Was the Dark Fae in cahoots with local witches? It didn't matter. We'd be gone soon enough. No point telling Morgan. She was edgy as it was. I couldn't dismantle the bags, but I dropped a barrier over them so they couldn't harm anyone.

"Quiet about these," I cautioned Zeke.

He rubbed his head against me. I took it as agreement.

When we walked through the door to our room, Morgan shot to her feet. "Where on earth were you? I was keeping an eye on everything, but you slid off my radar. There were a good ten minutes when I couldn't locate you."

I kicked the door shut, set the cold coffee and goodies on the table, and opened my arms. She ran into them and hugged me.

"I felt the oddest thing," Zeke told her. *"Magic was deployed, trolling for me. Once it latched on, it wouldn't let go until I made certain we all ended up at an illusory cottage."*

"Illusory, how?" Morgan let go of me and asked.

Mmph. I'd been pretty sure it wasn't real. Zeke just confirmed it.

"Zeke led us to a cottage with a dark Fae. I didn't recognize her, and she wasn't all there mentally."

"Curious. What did she want?"

"To warn Damien," Sita chirped.

Morgan frowned. "About what?"

"She told me not to go, that bad things would happen if I did."

"Not to go where?"

"Same thing I asked," I replied, "but she didn't answer."

Morgan clasped her hands in front of her and rested her chin on them. "Maybe you're not supposed to hunt for Hecate with me."

I blew out a breath. "Might be what she meant, but I'm not about to change plans on the word of a raving lunatic, magic or no."

"Did she say anything else?" Morgan dropped her arms to her sides.

"Return to Faery before it's too late," Sita cawed.

"No specifics?" Morgan pressed.

I shook my head. "None. Dark Fae are meddlesome creatures. They have incredibly strong magical ability. For some, it's so robust they're not sure what to do with it, and the indecision drives them mad."

"Maybe we shouldn't discount her warning. After all, Zeke was drawn to her."

I walked to the table and grabbed a cup of coffee, handing it to Morgan. "We're going to slug down this brew, eat a few of the bakery items, and leave. The only question is whether we go to Lagina or the two islands you're catching visions of."

"Ikaria and Samos?"

"The same." I broke a croissant stuffed with ham and cheese in half and offered it to her.

She took a bite, chewed, swallowed. "Any way I can talk you into sitting this one out?"

"Nope."

"I don't believe in coincidences." She finished the rest of her half of the croissant.

"Neither do I. And serendipity is a crock."

"Then why aren't you taking the dark Fae seriously?"

I resisted a desire to laugh. "I've never taken any dark Fae seriously. Not about to start now."

She rustled in the bakery sack and extracted a cheese Danish. I grabbed one filled with cherries and my cup of coffee.

It didn't take long to finish breakfast.

I chucked my cup and the sack into the trash. "Which will it be? Lagina or the islands?"

Morgan ran the heels of her hands down her cheeks. "Damn it. I just don't know. Not sure it matters. If one well is dry, we'll look down the other."

In a normal world, with normal rules, I'd have agreed with her. While I didn't believe in the dark Fae's warning, what had sunk in was we were running out of time. Darkness surrounded us, cropping up with greater and greater frequency.

I wrapped an arm around her shoulders. "Because you're seeing them, I vote for the islands. We can start on Ikaria."

"Have you been there before?"

I stopped to think about it before answering, "Yes, but it was so long ago, nothing will be the same."

Morgan glanced at Zeke. "You're who the Fae connected with. What do you think?"

The wolf shook himself. *"Danger stalks us. Whatever we do needs to be done quickly."*

Surprise tightened my muscles. Zeke's take mirrored mine. I summoned a journey spell and draped it over us all.

"Hold up." Morgan ducked from under my arm and retrieved her bag from the armoire. I'd forgotten about it. Nothing else of ours here.

To be on the safe side, I obliterated all traces of us just before my spell swept us away.

CHAPTER FIFTEEN,
MORGAN

Hot water hitting my body felt ambrosial. Everywhere it touched reminded me of licks or kisses or strokes. Lovemaking had been so off-the-charts, I lacked words to describe the soft, glowy sensations teasing every nerve, every cell. If I'd had any idea what I was missing, I'd never have bought into the Coven's enforced celibacy.

Maybe if I'd had a series of liaisons, though, my time with Damien wouldn't have been so precious.

Cuts both ways.

The Coven's rationale regarding "no men" was crystal clear. We were supposed to place loyalty to our Coven above everything. Witches infatuated with men—or their cocks— would only get in the way of witchy business.

Was this one of Hecate's edicts?

The thought stopped me cold. I wasn't about to give up

Damien for anyone. Not even her. Surely, after all this time, there'd be room for compromise.

Why would there be? Coven rules didn't have a shred of wiggle room.

Well, if she wants me, she's going to have to bend.

Not very fucking likely given my limited experience with deities. It was their way or the highway.

I stopped trying to control an unknown future, grabbed a towel, dried off, and got back into my clothes. They were overkill for either of our proposed destinations, which would be hot and tropical. No help for it. I could toss my jacket over my shoulders. Or tie it around my waist.

I'd been checking on my family. My current scan couldn't locate them. Heart hammering against my chest, I looked again. Still nothing. What had gone wrong? Should I hunt for them? What if they ran into trouble?

I consulted an old-fashioned analog clock sitting on the dresser. If I couldn't find them ten minutes from now, I'd set spells in motion and leave. The last time I'd done that, it had taken Damien and I days to reconnect. Better to wait a short while in case something unknown had blocked the flow of my seeking spell.

Another towel sopped up drips from my hair. I braided it to get it out of the way. Concern for Damien and my familiars gnawed at me. They'd been gone a long while for a potty break.

One more quick check with magic located them. Relief spilled through me. I'd been more worried than I realized.

Damn it. I had to get hold of myself. Nerves weren't attractive on anyone, and they'd never been my style. I settled into a chair, got up, sat again. Finally, I made a grab for Damien's phone and did some mindless scrolling.

I'd have felt better going after Hecate alone. Zeke and Sita were my weak spots, and now Damien was another.

What in the unholy godhead was I doing traipsing into the unknown with everyone I held dear? Mother hadn't asked me to watch over Sita, but it was what she would have wanted. Her last few days hadn't been conducive to much of anything. She'd been mired in witchy spells that had gained enough momentum to kill her.

If I'd known, could I have done anything to subvert them?

Probably not. Fae healers are famous for their skill, and they'd proven helpless in the face of Mother's difficulties. About the only thing they did was provide the first clue to my origins by telling me Mother and I weren't related. Not by blood, anyway.

The door swung open about the same time Sita flew through the still open window. Damien had a cardboard carrier with two cups and a bakery bag. I shot to my feet. "Where on earth were you? I was keeping an eye on everything, but you slid off my radar. There were a good ten minutes when I couldn't locate you."

Damien set down his bounty and opened his arms, I rushed into them savoring the solid feel of him against me.

"Sorry, didn't mean to worry you." Damien's hold on me tightened. I wrapped my arms around him digging my fingertips into the weave of his jacket.

"Not Damien's fault. I felt the oddest thing," Zeke said. *"Magic was deployed, trolling for me. Once it latched on, it*

wouldn't let go until I made certain we all ended up at an illusory cottage."

"Illusory, how?" Alarmed, I let go of Damien. The place he'd been pressed against me felt suddenly cold.

"Zeke led us to a strange out-of-sync cottage with a dark Fae. I didn't recognize her, and she wasn't all there mentally," Damien explained.

"Curious. What did she want?"

"To warn Damien," Sita chirped.

I frowned. "About what?"

"She told me not to go, that bad things would happen if I did," he said.

"Not to go where?"

"Same thing I asked," Damien replied, "but she didn't answer."

Damn, damn, damn. This was playing right into my fears from earlier and my intuitive sense I should go alone.

"It has to be about Hecate," I murmured. "I need to do this alone."

"Like hell, you are. I'm not about to change plans on the word of a raving lunatic, magic or no," Damien growled.

"Did she say anything else?" I sucked in a tense breath.

"Return to Faery before it's too late," Sita cawed.

"No specifics?" I pressed.

Damien shook his head. "None. Dark Fae are meddlesome creatures. They have incredibly strong magical ability. For some, it's so robust they're not sure what to do with it, and the indecision drives them mad."

"Maybe we shouldn't discount her warning. After all, Zeke was drawn to her."

Damien handed me a cup of coffee. "We're going to slug down this brew, eat a few of the bakery items, and leave. The only question is whether we go to Lagina or the two islands you're catching visions of."

I ate part of a croissant. I should have been hungry, but it was dry and tasteless. "Any way I can talk you into sitting this one out?"

"Nope."

"I don't believe in coincidences."

"Neither do I. And serendipity is a crock."

"Then why aren't you taking the dark Fae seriously?" I demanded.

"I've never taken any dark Fae seriously. Not about to start now."

"Perhaps you're underestimating them."

He ignored my comment.

"Which will it be? Lagina or the islands?" he asked once we were done eating.

"Damn it. I just don't know. Not sure it matters. If one well is dry, we'll look down the other."

Damien wrapped an arm around my shoulders. "Because you're seeing them, I vote for the islands. We can start on Ikaria."

"Have you been there before?"

He paused. "Yes, but it was so long ago, nothing will be the same."

I glanced at Zeke. "You're who the Fae connected with. What do you think?"

"Danger stalks us. Whatever we do needs to be done quickly."

Damien summoned a journey spell and draped it over us all.

"Hold up." I ducked from under my arm and retrieved my bag from the armoire, slinging it over a shoulder. Damien scattered enchantment to obliterate any trace we'd ever been here. Why was he being so cautious? What did he know that I didn't?

His casting swept us away. The hotel room shattered, replaced by the darkness of a travel channel.

"You're quiet," Damien murmured.

May as well be upfront about my misgivings. "I don't have good feelings about this."

"Is it because of the dark Fae?"

"And other things."

"She was a raving lunatic. I recognize the type," he said in an effort to be reassuring.

I turned to glance at him. "Raving lunatic or not, she was together enough to draw Zeke to her."

Damien shrugged. "Magic calls to its own."

"Then why not you? Or Sita? Or me?" The more we talked, the more jittery I became.

"You were inside behind shielding."

"Fine. Maybe not me. But you're sidestepping my point." I checked his spell. We were nearly to Ikaria. I'm not especially well-traveled considering how long I've been alive. Remaining in the Coven guild house had always been sufficient.

Shortsighted of me. If I'd seen more of the world, I would have been better prepared for life on the run.

Damien's spell altered to include invisibility. Wise of him. If I weren't so spun out, I'd have done it myself.

The salt smell of the sea, heat, and cloying humidity surrounded us. People were everywhere, many of them in bathing suits, a few fully nude. Surf pounded against a nearby shore. From the angle of the sun, it was late afternoon.

Damien herded us away from the beach to a narrow street lined with buildings that may have dated back to the 1700s. Somehow, he located a deserted alley where we set ourselves to rights with our respective glamours.

The only one traveling *au naturel* was Sita. I had no idea if hawks like her were common in the Greek Islands. Hopefully, we wouldn't be here long enough to arouse commentary.

From anyone.

"Where do you think we should start?" I asked Damien.

"*I can sniff out witches,*" Zeke, back in his Aussie glamour, offered.

"The western end of the island used to have a cave system," Damien said.

"And?"

"You caught a glimpse of the tourists. I have a tough time envisioning Hecate hobnobbing with a bunch of half-naked mortals."

My mouth twitched into a smile. "I don't know her well enough to predict her behavior. Neither do you."

"*I still like my sniffing idea best,*" Zeke said. "*Or you can do your tracking spell.*"

I'd considered using magic but hadn't wanted to give

away our position until I was more certain of how I'd be received—if I found her. Perhaps I was being overly cautious.

We sidled out of the narrow slot between buildings and joined the throngs wandering this way and that.

HOURS PASSED. The only magical creatures on Ikaria were us. The cave Damien remembered was no more. Sea water filled it. Dusk had ceded to night by the time we gave up and moved on to Samos. Perhaps because it was night, fewer people wandered about. It appeared this island wasn't quite as popular a tourist landing spot.

Zeke had begun grumbling about being hungry.

"But you just ate before we left Northern England," I reminded him.

"That was hours ago. And I didn't get much because of the dark Fae."

Oh yeah. Her. So far, Damien was still in one piece. Her warning likely only applied if we managed to locate Hecate. It was a sure bet she wasn't on the hunt for me.

Why did I even care? Far more satisfying to wreak havoc on the Coven that had exiled me. Once that was accomplished, I could move on to helping witches escape black magic.

I have to care, I answered myself. *Because of Mother. She gave up everything to preserve the secret of my making.*

We weren't as thorough as we trolled through Samos's few streets. Much like Ikaria, all the cities bordered the sea.

Buildings dotted mountains rising from beach level. We covered the north side of the island first before moving to its southerly shores.

In the wee small hours of morning, we stood on Limnonaki's white sand beaches no closer to an answer than we'd been when we left Carlisle. I moved the strap of my bag to the other side and shoved hair over my shoulders.

Under cover of darkness, both Zeke and Sita had located game. Probably not enough to satisfy Zeke, but something was better than nothing. I was hungry too, but it wasn't a major distraction yet.

"I don't understand why this path turned into a dry hole," Damien muttered. "Why were you seeing this place if not to guide us?"

I shrugged. "Who knows... Damn it. Could have been here all along."

"What could have?" he and Zeke asked in synchrony. Sita was perched in a tree digging bugs out of its bark.

Pointing to the pounding surf, I said, "The Mer people. They have to be here too. They've helped me before, and not much gets past them."

"You could have hobnobbed with them in the North Sea," Damien pointed out. "Or the Irish one."

"Maybe the ones who live here would know more, though." Not wanting to repeat the mistake of getting my clothing soaked, I hunkered in the lee of a large boulder and started undressing, tucking each item beneath smaller rocks, so they wouldn't blow away.

Damien took off his jacket.

"Uh-uh," I said. "Someone needs to keep an eye on Zeke and Sita."

"What did you do with them the other times?"

Down to my underwear, I began to shiver. Even the tropics cool off in the dead of night. Not the best time to argue about this. "Once they came with me. It limited my time underwater. The next time, I left them, but that was before they were kidnapped."

He opened his mouth. Before he could launch a rationale for why he needed to stick to me like glue, I said. "This is nonnegotiable. Besides, it's the last card left in the deck. If it doesn't pan out, we have to move on." Leaving my panties in place—they'd dry on my body—I sprinted for the surf.

Thank the goddess he didn't ignore my wishes—more like an edict—and join me. Water encased my legs. When it hit waist level, I dove into the warm salt water and opened my mind voice to call the Mer people.

A mermaid with turquoise hair tangled with seaweed met me about fifty yards from shore. "We've been expecting you." Silver eyes crinkled at the corners when she smiled.

"Why?"

"We sensed your presence. Who else would you turn to? No other magic-wielder maintains a presence on these islands. Only in the sea."

Alrighty. Expecting me because they were the only game in town had a whole different flavor than expecting me because they had information to impart.

"Come. Our regent is waiting."

She dove for the depths. I swam after her, fine-tuning my ability to extract oxygen from water. I'd expected a castle. Instead, we followed a trajectory straight out to sea. The water temperature dropped until I diverted a thin flow of magic to keep myself warm. When we got to a spot she must have recognized, she angled downward, not stopping until we came to the ocean floor.

Small phosphorescent fish swam past, lighting the murky depths.

A Merman joined us. Silvery hair floated around him. Green eyes examined me. A light touch brushed my magical center. I hadn't thought to guard it. Too late now. A hasty ward would be rude, indicate I lacked trust.

I was on their turf. If they meant me harm, no ward in the world would save me.

"Welcome to our realm." The man extended a hand. I clasped it.

"Appreciate your hospitality," I said.

"Someone wishes an audience with you," the man informed me.

My stomach tightened. I treaded water to remain in place, while brushing debris out of the way.

Water rippled as something large approached. Neither of the Mer people exhibited concern. Blinking I peered through the gloom. A triangular head roughly the size of Zeke came into view. Sinuous coils paid out behind it.

Shock punched me in the guts.

A kraken.

I've seen them in books, but never in the flesh. Unsure of protocol, I bowed low and waited.

"Up, up," he growled amidst a stream of bubbles. No mind speech for him—or perhaps it was a her.

I raised my head.

The beast moved until its head was even with mine. Its scales were gray-green. White eyes were mounted on the sides of its head. Heavy lids covered them. I remained still as he examined me.

After a time, he nodded once. The movement of his huge head created a cascade of ripples.

"I am here at Hecate's behest. You will come with me."

I'd been a trusting soul before the sisterhood ousted me. As things stood, I trusted no one. *"Why isn't she here? Why send you?"*

"Does it matter?" he rumbled.

"Yes, it does. My...friends are back on the beach. I'm not going anywhere without them."

"You came here," he pointed out.

"Merely on a fact gathering mission." I hesitated before testing the waters. *"We could all accompany you so long as most of the journey isn't underwater."*

"She only requested you."

The beast's coils were undulating faster now. Had I pissed him off? First off, he might only be saying he was Hecate's emissary. I'd be nine kinds of stupid to follow blindly.

An idea surfaced. I erected what I hoped was subtle shielding, so no one would question the truth of my next words. Smiling to underscore what an upstanding witch I am, I said, *"Okay. Be happy to come along, but first I need to return to the beach and inform my companions what I'm doing. If I don't, Damien will worry so much he might drag in the entire Fae army to find where I went."*

"Use telepathy," the creature suggested.

Oops, hadn't considered that angle. *"I would, but we've had such a rough go of it lately, Damien won't believe me unless he lays eyes on me."*

I glanced from the Mer people to the Kraken, keeping my breathing nice and easy. Would they fall for my gambit?

If they didn't, would I have to fight my way back to the beach? If I screamed for Damien once my head broke the surface, he'd come at a dead run. So would Zeke and Sita.

The beast swung his mighty head from side to side. For all I knew, he was conversing with Hecate—or whoever'd really sent him.

"Be quick about it," he growled.

It took a moment before it sank in my ploy had paid off. Bowing low, I murmured, *"Thank you,"* and struck out swimming for the surface. I'd finish the distance from there to where I'd left everyone with my head above the waves.

Neither of the Mer people followed me. I'd been afraid they would to ensure I kept my word, a promise I had every intention of breaking.

Shit. I was collecting enemies like some women collect high heels.

Water sheeted off me as I broke through the surface and set a course for shore. I was a good mile or more out. I started to alert Damien but decided not to in case someone intercepted the telepathy I'd said I couldn't use.

To shorten things up, I wound magic into a tiny jump spell that landed me near where I'd left my clothes. Bending, I gathered everything into my arms.

"What happened?" Damien was next to me in a trice, along with Zeke and Sita.

"Summon a travel spell. Get us out of here now," I panted.

Thank the goddess he didn't waste time questioning me. Neither did he ask where we were going. The smells of an evergreen forest surrounded me as the beach shuddered into motes of light.

Still clutching my clothes and boots, I leaned against him shivering. We were safe. For now.

But we were running out of places to hide. "Where are we going?" I asked through chattering teeth.

"Faery." His tone was grim. "Do not say another word until we're there. Her barriers will ensure no one listens in."

Zeke pressed against me, licking water off my skin. Sita perched on a shoulder, stroking her beak against my cheek.

I blanked out my mind and swathed us in layers of protection.

Would I ever feel safe again anywhere?

I doubted it. Misery descended. For all my pretty words about pity parties and how worthless they were, I dove headfirst into one, wallowing in its depths.

CHAPTER SIXTEEN, DAMIEN

I'd just begun to worry about Morgan when she rolled onto the beach next to her stack of garments. One look at her convinced me things had gone horribly wrong. My journey spell was well on its way, even before she requested one.

"What happened?" Zeke asked me as he came at a run.

"I don't know, and we're not going to talk about anything until it's safe," I told the wolf. If Morgan heard either of us, she didn't give any indication.

Faery's barriers parted, allowing us entry. For once, Maeve wasn't waiting at the gates with her crystal ball. I whisked us to my rooms before stopping long enough for Morgan to towel off and crawl back into her clothes.

After handing her a goblet of aged mead, I waited for her to pony up an explanation. At least, she'd stopped shivering.

After draining half the glass, she said, "I'm not sure quite what happened under the sea, but it felt odd. Not right."

"Details," Zeke woofed, the word more-or-less understandable.

I gave him kudos for the same question I'd have asked.

Morgan nodded. I pointed to an upholstered chair, but she murmured, "Too wound up to sit." Still hanging onto the mead, she paced from one end of my two-room suite to the other.

"A mermaid met me," she began. "She said she'd been expecting me, which didn't seem too unusual. The Mer people keep tabs on everything magical in their jurisdictions."

So far, it sounded innocuous. "Then what?" I didn't want to rush her, but we needed to get the salient points out on the table before some unknown enemy stormed Faery's gates.

"I followed her. It was a long way. Miles. We reached a spot where she dove straight to the ocean floor. A Merman met us there. Said he was regent for this group and that someone was here to meet me."

Oh-oh. Innocuous was giving way to worrisome. I bit back a flurry of words aimed at dragging her tale out of her.

Morgan drained her glass and held it out for a refill. I obliged, but she set it on a table once it was full. "Getting drunk won't make this go away," she mumbled before going on. "The someone who swam out of the gloom was a kraken."

I whistled long and low. I've only seen one, and it was centuries ago.

"*What's that?*" Zeke asked.

Touching his shoulder, I sent an image into his mind. It

elicited a burst of yips. *"Like a dragon but without wings,"* he growled.

"That lives beneath the sea," I added.

Morgan took a few more sips of mead. "The kraken said Hecate had sent him to bring me to her." Her forehead furrowed in thought. "Except I didn't exactly believe him. Something didn't feel right. He was insistent we leave right away."

Alarm soured my stomach. "How'd you escape?"

She grimaced. "I, erm, lied. First I said I wanted to bring you and the animals with me to Hecate. The kraken vetoed it. Next, I said I needed to make a quick trip to the beach to let you know where I was going."

I fell back a step. Kraken are rumored to be wise and quite intelligent. "He fell for it?"

"Yeah, surprised me too. I tried to be subtle crafting a ward around my mind so he couldn't glean my thoughts, but still..."

"What made you suspicious of his intentions?"

She shrugged. "I've never read about a sea monster being part of anything witchlike. Also, Hecate created Zeke along with me. Why wouldn't she want both of us? My instincts might be working overtime, but the whole situation felt bogus."

"Any reason the Mer people would screw you?"

"None I can think of, but the kraken is a fellow ocean-dweller. Maybe it counts for more than whatever relationship I have with them."

"Or they might have taken his words at face value," I mused. "Why would they have reason to doubt him."

"How do you know it's a him?"

"They all are," I told her. "They don't reproduce. The gods created about six of them eons ago."

"I see." After another generous slug, she set the glass down. "I'm grateful we're out of there, but I have no idea what to do next other than find a handy cave and wait out a few centuries to see if the heat dies down."

"Not sounding like the witch I love." Walking close, I dropped both hands on her shoulders, careful not to displace Sita, who hadn't budged.

Morgan turned her hands palms up. "What can we do? I'll be damned if I embroil the Fae army in my war. The only witch who was in my court was Mother. I'm not welcome in my home Coven. Probably not in any other, either, at this point.

"Oh, and don't forget the curse."

"We don't know if it's even real," I reminded her, troubled by how dejected she was.

"What avenues do you think are open?" She raised her mismatched gaze to meet mine.

"There's always a path forward."

"Not seeing it."

My door swung open. Maeve and Logan marched in. "Told you they were back," Maeve said.

Zeke ran to them, tail wagging enthusiastically.

"How about if I give you some privacy?" Morgan skirted around them, heading for the still-open door.

"Stay put," Maeve ordered.

Morgan spun, an incredulous expression on her face. "I am not Fae. You do not get to tell me what to do."

"Don't be rude," Zeke woofed.

"Gods, is no one on my side?" Morgan bolted out the door. Zeke and Sita remained in my rooms.

I started after Morgan, but Maeve said, "Let her go. Probably good to run off all that adrenaline."

I stopped beneath the lintel and turned to face her. "What do you know?" I asked without preamble.

"Most of what she probably just told you. I saw the kraken in my pool. He's up to no good and is definitely not working with Hecate."

"Then, who sent him?"

"Hard to say." The seer set her mouth in a tight line. "My guess would be the witches who are still trying to corral Morgan. Or the Kelpies or Banshees or demons they're in cahoots with, but witches get my first vote."

"Do you think the Kraken was being used?" Logan asked.

Maeve shot a glance his way. "Why would you ask that?"

"Because they're respectable creatures. Throughout history, they've fought dark magic, not embraced it."

Interesting. Logan had just shed a whole new light on things. Perhaps it was why the Mer people had been part of an unwitting plot to snare Morgan.

"Krakens are also intelligent," Maeve reminded him.

"Aye, that they are. I can see a group of witches approaching him, telling him they're emissaries from Hecate and in need of his assistance. It would have appealed to his chivalrous side."

"What would he have done when Morgan pitched a hissy fit after he escorted her to a group of witches?" I wondered.

"Depends whom he believed," Maeve said.

"What will you do now?" Logan asked.

"Morgan wants to throw in the towel and hide in a cave somewhere."

"Oh, she does, does she?" Maeve arched white brows. "She doesn't have that luxury."

Protectiveness surged. "Why not?"

"Balls are in play. They will reach a natural conclusion with or without her cooperation. 'Tis far better if she's an active participant. She may not like the outcome if she gives up."

Seers are famous for doubletalk. "What, exactly, does that mean?"

"I was clear enough." She sniffed and waved a dismissive hand.

"You could add a wee bit more," Logan suggested.

"Like what?"

"Which balls are in play?" I asked.

She blew a breath out and held up a hand, counting on her fingers. "One. Hecate is loose. Two. She has to be plotting revenge. Three. She will come for Morgan sooner or later. Four. Witches around the world are falling prey to evil. Do I need to go on?"

"Yes, please do," I said.

"I've already told you my crystals have run red with blood and are now turning black if I dig too deep. War will find us all. It's not a matter of if, but when."

"What role does Morgan play?" Pulling teeth would have been simpler, cleaner.

"Why, she's the lynchpin, and, as her mate, you're right

there in the eye of the storm with her."

"What's a lynchpin?" Zeke woofed.

"Something that causes something," Maeve told him.

"Morgan didn't cause anything," Zeke protested.

"Yes," Sita cawed. "Witches treated her like dirt."

"I didn't mean it was her fault," Maeve clarified. "Just that she's at the center of this magical storm, whether she wants to be there or not."

"I heard all that." Morgan trudged back into my rooms.

"Of course, you did," Logan said.

"I'm done feeling sorry for myself." Rolling her shoulders back, she stood tall. "I'm ready to find Hecate, but I'm going alone."

"Bad idea." Maeve shook a finger at her.

"I second that," Logan said.

Since Morgan would go alone over my dead body—but it sounded heavy-handed as fuck—I waited to see which way the wind would blow.

"You are not going anywhere without me," Zeke announced. Defiance streamed from him.

"Or me," Sita cawed.

"Don't you see?" Morgan spread her hands in front of her. "I need to do this alone because I love you. Putting myself at risk is one thing—"

"We won't stand by and let you march into danger alone." Hackles raised the length of Zeke's spine.

"Look what happened to Zoelle." Sita sounded frantic. "I cannot lose another witch. Will not, not while I have a beak and wings."

"I have seen you together, not apart," Maeve observed.

"So? What you see often doesn't come to pass," Morgan retorted.

"In this instance, where every single viewing has the four of you together, I take my future seeing seriously."

Logan hooked an arm through Maeve's. "Let's leave them alone, shall we? They have plans to develop." On his way out, he called, "Faery's resources stand behind you, although I hope to Danu you do not have to call upon them."

The door swung shut, leaving us by ourselves.

Morgan sank into the chair she'd refused earlier and dropped her face into her hands, rubbing her temples.

"We're going about this all wrong," she mumbled.

I perched on the arm of her chair. The animals moved next to us. "How so?"

"We could search for her for months, years even. Somehow, I have to draw her to me."

"How?" I stopped there. If Hecate wanted to claim her minion, she'd had ample chance.

Morgan's lips parted in a parody of a smile. "I'll start showing up at Covens claiming sovereignty."

"Bold. Now, tell me what you're really considering."

Within the folds of a pointed look, she retorted, "I just did."

Not wanting to blurt out it was maybe not the worst idea ever, but close to it, I probed, asking for details.

She perched on the edge of the chair and faced me. "You'll recall I had no trouble mowing through five witches. I barely tapped into my current skills."

"You're going to go in, guns blazing, and kill whomever stands in your way?"

"Only the ones turned to evil. They're not a loss to anyone."

"I like it," Zeke woofed enthusiastically, tail pluming.

"Yes. We'll kill the ones who murdered Zoelle," Sita shrieked. "I can't wait to sink my beak into their eyeballs and necks."

Damn it. This was getting worse and worse. "How will you tell who's who?"

The jaunty angle of her shoulders drooped a bit. "It's the only weak spot. I may end up destroying a few innocents. Can't be helped."

What happened to the sweet, shy, naïve witch who'd stumbled into my boardinghouse in Seattle? She'd been cold and hungry and so devastated by circumstances, she was malleable.

"She's long gone." Morgan's words could have etched stone. Standing, she crossed her arms beneath her breasts. "I've been hounded, chased, cursed. My familiars have been kidnapped. I'm sick to death of every witch who fell headlong into the rhetoric I was a problem and needed to be destroyed. They have to get over themselves. It's long past time."

I blew out a breath. "Okay. How is this new slash-and-burn motif going to get you closer to Hecate?"

"Simple," she informed me in a tone that suggested I was brain dead not to have picked up on the connection straight away. "I'll tell each Coven I'm Hecate's emissary, that my actions are dictated by her orders. Word will get back to her, and she'll come at a dead run."

"Yes, and she'll be furious. Any chance you might have had to work together will be pounded to dust."

Twin vertical lines formed between Morgan's brows. "It's the oddest thing."

"What?" I prodded.

"Lately, since I ran from the Kraken, I've seen a woman in my mind's eye. It could be Hecate, or it might be someone else."

"What does she look like?" Not that I'd recognize the witch goddess by sight, but I could relay a visual to Maeve, who might know more.

"She's tall. My height, but skin-stretched-over-bones gaunt. Black hair would probably reach the floor were it not in braids. Her eyes are copper colored with green pupils. The times she's appeared, she's worn a black silk robe embroidered with golden runes and leather sandals."

"Did she say anything?" I pressed.

Morgan shook her head. "It felt as if she wanted to, was trying to, but something got in the way. Each time she came to me, the vision ended abruptly."

"How many times?"

"Three. It's only been a handful of hours since we fled Samos, but she keeps knocking on the gates of my mind."

Trying to reason rather than react, I posed my question carefully. "Do you suppose your idea to burn down the Covens has anything to do with those visitations?"

Morgan's eyes widened. She dropped he arms to her sides. "Crap. Am I being manipulated even absent her saying anything? I don't get it. Most witches still worship her."

I marshaled my thoughts before continuing. "If your

visitor is Hecate, and I'm not seeing who else it could be, she'd have a strong link with you even over distance. Perhaps she was captured again and is being held against her wishes—"

"But everyone says she broke free."

"Aye. Naught says her enemies didn't gang up and nab her again. According to Hermes, they were all over it." I lapsed into Gaelic, something I tend to do when I'm puzzling through a conundrum.

Morgan's mouth twisted into a grimace. "Is she like me? No allies?"

"You have us." Zeke head butted her.

"Of course, I do, dear heart. And the Fae. Sorry. Didn't mean to offend. What I meant was the gods and witches are still plotting to take her down."

Leaving the topic of whether Hecate was, once again, a prisoner, I asked, "Have you thought how you'd finesse taking the first Coven?"

"Not really." She made a sour face. "The best defense is a good offense, so I'll blow through the door, storm inside, and announce I am there as Hecate's agent. Keeping it short and sweet, I'll say she's worried witches are falling prey to evil, and she sent me to root them out."

"By then, they'll have joined power and laid an entrapment casting," I pointed out.

"Not if I'm careful. I'll have Zeke and Sita. Legends of a witch with two familiars will be heavy on everyone's mind. They'll think twice before attacking."

"What if you're wrong?"

"Then we'll come out swinging. I'll pick a couple of

obvious targets, ones whose auras are black. Shouldn't take more than a few deaths to bring the rest of the Coven to heel."

"But they'll hate you."

She tossed her head. "So what? I'm doing a service for—"

Pain and isolation sluiced from her in waves. Seeing her suffering smote me. On my feet, I drew her into my arms. "We'll figure something out. It might look a lot like what you just said, but I don't want you to have many more deaths on your conscience."

"I'll kill for her," Sita cawed.

"And me," Zeke woofed.

Stiff at first, Morgan relaxed against me.

"If Hecate is being held against her will again," I said softly, "she won't be able to show up no matter what hell you raise at Coven central."

"Maybe it will give her enough strength to break the barrier holding us apart," Morgan insisted.

In an attempt to settle one unknown, I called out to Maeve, *"Are you sure Hecate's still free?"*

After a lengthy pause, she replied, *"No. Let me look into it."*

"So it could be her," Morgan murmured.

"Try this," I suggested. "Next time you see her, open a channel and follow it. But tell me, I want to be there."

"Why didn't I think of that?" She untangled herself from my embrace. "These sightings happen quickly. What if you're not around?"

"Find me."

"By then, she'll be gone." Morgan sucked in a tense breath, eyes widening. "Speak of the devil. It's her again."

I made a grab for her hand. "Go after her in the psychic space. Do it now."

"But what about—?"

"Now," I insisted. "While you can follow the energy."

Determination twisted Morgan's features into harsh planes.

A strong wind nearly jerked me off my feet. The familiar suite of rooms shattered, replaced by a barren plain with hundred-mile-an-hour winds scouring it. A distant mountain range was illuminated by a setting sun. If I hadn't been hanging onto Morgan, she'd have been jerked away.

Zeke's howls and Sita's strident caws faded. They were safe in Faery, but where in the hell were we? The landscape bore a passing relationship to at least one of Maeve's visions.

Strain carved lines in Morgan's face. Hair whipped behind her. "Not long now," she cried.

I barely heard her over the shriek of the wind.

In a last-ditch effort to be prepared, I latched onto her magical center with my own. We were stronger together, but my move held risks. More for me than her. Assuming we were heading into a witch-spawned maelstrom, they could reach me through Morgan, carve me up, and feed me to the kraken.

Not going to happen.

This was my idea. It had come to me because it was sound. The better half of magic is believing in it—and yourself. Weaving protections around us both, I waited. We had to come out the far side of this soon.

I aimed to be ready.

CHAPTER SEVENTEEN, MORGAN

When Damien suggested going after my elusive visitor, it had sounded like a grand idea. Now I wasn't so certain. Bringing the familiars into this unknown territory had been out of the question. While I hated leaving them alone, they should be protected by Faery.

I hoped.

Wind wanted to rip me end for end. Its infernal screeching filled every space in my mind, soul, and heart. A few witches have always been weather-workers; I searched for the telltale signs we'd been nabbed by the sisterhood.

Not my sisterhood, a sour inner voice piped up.

Music, haunting and evocative, played urging me to follow it. "Can you hear that?" I shouted, but Damien didn't answer. If the poignant melody was only for me, it stank of coercion.

Where were we going? Had someone laid a trap, and

we'd walked right into it? My breath was snatched away by the wind. Resolved not to be anybody's patsy—after all, I'd dragged Damien into this, or he'd dragged himself—I stretched my mind voice.

"Who are you?"

"You're smarter than that."

"Maybe not. Answer the question, or we're leaving."

"What makes you think you can?"

Aw crap. If I hadn't been so immersed in fighting the wind and ignoring the swell of notes pounding my ears, I might have worried.

"Keep after her," Damien urged. Wise of him not to use telepathy. It would be intercepted.

I'd been stretched out, belly down, providing less resistance as we skimmed several feet above ground level. To make the point that I was still in control, I adopted an upright position. Damien mirrored my movements. It slowed us quite a bit.

"What do you want from me?" I tried another tack.

"You are mine. Come home to me, child. Lend me your power." Jabs battered my magical center on the heels of her words.

"No fucking way."

"Show some respect. If not for me, you wouldn't exist." A pause, and then, *"Together, we could rule all worlds."*

Yeah, right. If she had that kind of ability, what did she need me for?

"Where are you?" May as well garner what information I could.

"Not far."

"Tells me nothing. Where?"

"Not sure."

Her words pinged sourly. Either she was in a great deal of pain, or she was lying. I voted for the latter.

The music was so loud, thinking became a challenge. "Can you hear that?" I shouted.

"Hear what?"

Fuck. I'd been afraid of that. "Never mind."

The wind altered, creating vortices that tried to sweep us into them.

"We have to leave." Damien spoke into my ear. I barely heard him above the incessant racket. No longer inviting and seductive, the music had morphed into a discordant cacophony.

"But we don't know anything. Not yet."

"Feels wrong to me."

The weave of his enchantment tightened where it slotted with mine forming a shell around our talent. Timely since one more vortex surrounded us pulling us downward. At least the noise in my head backed off a few notches.

I hunted for landmarks, so I could find this spot again, but our surroundings were fluid, ever-changing. The mountain range was gone. The sun had backed up to midheaven.

"I'm taking us out of here. Now." Damien announced.

"Nooooooo," pounded through my brain like a series of hot nails. If it was Hecate, that one word conveyed anguish and despair. How could I leave her? She needed me.

The music shifted, once again seductive, calming, reassuring.

"Do not fight me." Tension underscored Damien's words. "We've stayed too long."

"Don't leave me, child. You're my only hope."

I was being ripped in two. My maker, my creator was in dire straits. Without me, she'd sink into oblivion, her power extinguished forever. If that happened, mine would wane as well until nothing remained...

The familiar scent of Fae enchantment bubbled as Damien did his damnedest to extricate us. I'm stronger than he is, but ambivalence intruded, paralyzing me.

"Morgan!" My name carried desperation. "Think of Zeke. Of Sita. If you don't jump on this train and lend your skill, you'll never see them again."

"The Fae lies. All of them do. Get rid of him. He stands between us."

Between Damien's exhortation and her blanket repudiation of the Fae, I came back to myself, found my strength and my ability to make my own decisions. Leaning into Damien, I poured fuel into his casting.

Even with my power, it was nip and tuck. We hung suspended, buffeted by ever-stronger winds for far too long. The music ceased abruptly. It should have been a relief, except it might bode something far worse in the offing.

When honey fails to work, people haul out the big guns.

"This is ridiculous," I muttered and opened every scrap of magic in my arsenal. Still, minutes ticked past before the ungodly barren world exploded, landing us where we'd begun. In Damien's rooms.

Zeke launched himself at me, knocked me to the ground,

and stood with his paws on my shoulders. *"You will never, never do that again,"* he snarled, full fangs on display.

"May shame fall upon your house," Sita shrieked, flying around the room like a mad thing. "Your mother would be appalled."

"Noted," I mumbled. "Sorry. Didn't mean to leave you. It just happened."

"Do. Not. Lie," Zeke snarled. *"If you'd meant to include us, you'd have draped your spell around us."*

"I wanted you to be safe."

"We feel the same way about you, but we can't protect you when you ditch us," Sita squawked disconsolately.

Zeke let me up and trotted to Damien.

Damien sank into a crouch, breathing hard. "Crap, I didn't think we were going to make it out of there."

I hadn't, either, but now didn't seem the time to highlight how powerless we'd been. "Where were we?" I rasped. My throat was raw from the wind; it ached.

"The space between worlds."

"So, like a borderworld?"

He shook his head. "Psychic energy runs between every magical world. It has its own flow and cadence. Some mages utilize it to hasten travel to distant locations. Others use it to...to wage war from afar."

I pinched the bridge of my nose between my thumb and forefinger. "If you knew that, why'd you suggest we follow her?"

"There's more than one psychic space. Most are far more benign than the one we got sucked into."

"I see."

"What made you change your mind?" His question came out of left field.

"Huh?"

"Something happened before you gave it the full-court press so we could leave. What was it?" Green eyes drilled into me.

"Two things. You saying I'd never see Zeke and Sita again, and her saying all Fae were shit." I sank into a chair.

Zeke licked Damien. *"At least one of you thought about us."*

"We were both thinking about you," I tossed out. Turning to Damien, I said, "This is dangerous for you. She wants me to herself."

"Of course, she does."

I bristled. "What's that supposed to mean?"

Damien looked away.

"Whatever this is, tell me."

"You won't like it."

I avoided rolling my eyes. "I haven't liked much of anything since the Coven kicked me to the curb."

He rose to his feet, walked to me, and placed a hand on my shoulder. "She's manipulating you. I felt the shift in your magical center when you shook her off and came back to yourself."

"Did you hear the music?"

He shook his head.

I'd figured as much. "Why use me? All she'd have to do is show up and talk with me."

"She doesn't know that. Hermes must have prevailed, and she's trapped again. Her innate ability isn't enough to break free, so she's luring you."

I chewed my lower lip. "Another explanation is someone is using her. Maybe the gig is delivering me in exchange for her freedom."

Damien let go of me and punched a nearby wall, cursing in Gaelic.

"No matter which it is, I have to be careful."

"We need to be careful," he corrected me.

"Maybe if I could go to her alone—"

"No," he thundered. "Be reasonable. Even with two of us, we barely got out of that place."

"*What place?*" Zeke woofed.

"A bad place," I told him.

Sita was still scribing circles and crying mournfully. I'd wounded both of them. Badly. Clearly, another approach was in order.

"You asked about music," Damien probed. "What was it like?"

"At first, it made me feel like I was coming home to people who loved me. Then it changed, became strident before returning to how it was at first."

He narrowed his eyes. "Do witches use music to power spells?"

"Not usually."

"Mmph. Means it was someone else. Kelpies use music. They sing their victims into compliance."

I chewed my lower lip. My head hurt. Why was I pursuing this? It would be far simpler to get on with my life.

A life with Damien.

Sita lit on my shoulder, talons digging deep enough

blood trickled down my chest. "Do you want me to go away?"

Guilt cut deep. "Of course not. I love you."

"Then why did you leave us?"

"I had no idea where we were going."

After a couple of beak clacks, she cawed, "Not good enough."

"Probably not. It won't happen again."

"It might," Damien said.

The longer I sat, the surer I was I had to go back. Not the way we'd entered that space this time, but surreptitiously, assuming I could find the same spot absent guidance. It implied flying solo. No one in this room would agree, which meant I'd have to sneak off and cover my tracks.

Hecate made me for her own reasons. I had to close the loop or shut that door permanently. If her intentions had deteriorated—and it was looking like a sure bet—I needed to tell her to her face I wasn't anyone's rube. Not even hers. Times were different than they'd been when she formed me from her essence. Minions were far more malleable then.

"Morgan?" Damien was next to me. Had he said something else, but I'd been lost in thought and hadn't heard him?

"Just tired."

"Get some rest."

I angled my head to look up at him. "Where are you going?"

"To talk with Maeve and Logan. Maybe she'll know more than she did a while ago. Or be more willing to share old information."

On my feet, I kissed him, keeping it short and sweet. Him leaving would give me the opportunity I sought. If the goddess—not Hecate, but someone—was with me, I'd be back before he knew I'd left.

"Back soon," he murmured and kissed me again. "We'll catch a meal and figure out what to do next."

Feeling like nine kinds of toxic deceit, I watched the door close behind him. The imprint of his lips still warmed mine. What the fuck was wrong with me? When I looked within, the pressure to return to Hecate was stronger than ever.

Zeke positioned himself between me and the door, staring intently with his mismatched eyes. *What are you plotting?*

Getting rid of Damien was one thing. My familiars quite another. "You make it sound so diabolical."

I know you.

He did, indeed, maybe better than I knew myself.

Nothing would do but the truth. I'd trampled all over his loyalty once today. Sita clung to my shoulder. The only way she'd leave was by force. I couldn't do that to her, not after everything she'd lived through. Familiars and witches pair bond forever. No one within my purview had died and left their familiar—except Mother.

Deep in my soul, the same music from the psychic space—a soothing melody not the jarring mixture—started up again. How had it penetrated Faery's veils? Worse, it meant they knew where I was.

Of course they did. I'd shown up with a Fae. The leap from there to me being in Faery was so elementary an idiot could have made the association.

"Well?" Zeke woofed, not bothering with telepathy.

I reached to stroke him, but he shied away. Whoa. That was a first. I sank into a crouch to be at his level and said, "I'd considered returning to the bad place. It's dangerous for Damien, so, if I return, it should be by myself."

"Never going to happen." Zeke closed his jaws around my wrist. Not hard, but a reminder he was willing to go to the mat on this one.

"If you go, you will take us," Sita squawked. A none-too-gentle beak poke at the side of my forehead drew blood that dripped slowly.

The music swelled, urging me on, except I couldn't disappoint my familiars. Not again. I tried blocking out the music.

No dice.

"Please let go," I said.

"Why?" Zeke glared.

"Because I'm going to find a bed and fall into it. You're welcome to lay next to me."

Mollified, he opened his jaws but stuck close enough to spring into a spell if I was bold enough to lie to his face. My heart hurt. After all our years together, one unexpected move and my wolf, my heart, didn't trust me anymore.

I'd never truly considered how hard leaving the Coven was for him. His life had been upended right along with mine, but he'd never complained.

"I'm lucky to have both of you," I told them. "More than lucky. Blessed. Apologies for leaving you behind."

"And?" Zeke's tail plumed.

"And I won't do it again."

After a quick stop in the bathroom to splash cold water on my face and wash my hands, I sat on the edge of Damien's bed and removed my shoes and socks. I wasn't clean enough to slide beneath the covers, so I lay atop the duvet inhaling his pine forest scent.

Sita left my shoulder for the headboard. Zeke stretched out next to me. Sandwiched between them and Damien's alluring scent, I felt safe. Illusion or not, peace descended. I'd blown through scads of magic escaping from the psychic space.

When I shut my eyes, consciousness took a hike. Sort of.

I wandered through a convoluted series of deep canyons along a footpath that had crumbled to ruin in many spots. Between the rocky hillside to my right and a steep drop-off into a raging river on my left, I utilized magic to leap across the sketchy parts.

The air wasn't as pristine as I expected. In a weird throwback it smelled much like the psychic space had absent the howling wind. In my mind's eye, Zeke ran ahead of me, and Sita flew overhead.

They weren't taking any chances and had joined me in the dreamscape.

The track veered uphill away from the river. A spectral visitor, who looked a whole lot like the woman in my visions, waited at the top. I wasn't surprised or worried. This was the dream world. It wasn't real.

No one could attack me here. At least, I didn't believe they could.

Zeke stood between me and the woman. Her black robe fluttered in a light breeze. The golden runes glowed as if backlit. This time, her long hair had been braided with flowers and beads.

She stretched bony fingers my way. "We do not have much time, child."

"Are you Hecate?"

She nodded. "Now is a time to listen. Once they discover I am gone, they will snatch me back."

Zeke growled. Sita retreated to my shoulder, her beak clacking wildly.

"Who is they?"

"I said, listen."

"Fine. No more interruptions."

"They will do whatever is necessary to keep us away from one another. It was wise of you to leave before. They will destroy you if they can. We must find a way to join forces. Once we do, we will be unstoppable."

Her copper eyes lit with bloodthirsty enthusiasm, their green centers dilated. "We will kill them all, you and me." Her voice dropped to a stage whisper. "But we must be careful."

"Tell me where you are. Damien and I can free you."

Bitter laughter rolled from Hecate. "No one can free me. After I escaped my bonds, they doubled down. I may never be free again."

"Then I'm not understanding how we can work together."

Her demeanor changed, grew wary. "You are cursed. They keep telling me as much. How did you let that happen?"

"I didn't," I gritted.

"You're lying. I can't work with a liar." Her tone escalated, becoming shrill. "How could you have fallen so far, child?"

The rapid shifts from topic to topic made my headache worse. Her criticism stung.

And made me angry.

"Now, you look here. I've done the best I could working and living in a vacuum. If you don't like the way I turned out, you have no one but yourself to blame. Where were you all those years? You swore Mother to silence. I've had to work things out on my own, and—"

"Get rid of the Fae," she hissed. "He is in the way. Not part of my plan."

Fuck. She was mad. From freeing her to killing everyone to cursed to Damien. I was done here. Still, this was an opportunity to close the loop.

She was still talking. I cut in. "If you don't tell me where you are, I can't help you. If your position about Damien is intransigent, I can't help you. I'm not some moonstruck maiden willing to sacrifice my entire life on the altar of your needs.

"Up until recently, I had no idea you even existed. So, you have choices. I am willing to help, but on a combination of terms: yours and mine. Not only yours."

The air around her turned red. Fury rolled from her in waves. Zeke stood his ground, hackles at full mast, growling.

"How dare you—" she began.

"You said our time was short. Pick your poison, or we're out of here."

The same hellish laughter erupted. Forms danced around her. I wasn't waiting to see what they turned into.

Calling the strands of a casting into being, I instructed it to return us to the bed we'd left in Faery.

"I didn't give you permission to leave," Hecate shrilled.

"Too bad about that. I don't require your permission or your blessing. No one has controlled me since I was ten years old. I'm sure as hell not starting now."

Sticking around to argue might offer her leverage, so I motioned Zeke to my side and kindled my spell.

We fell backward into blackness, tumbling end over end. Zeke's howls and Sita's shrieks tore at my heart. What had I gotten us into? The journey back to Damien's bedroom should have taken seconds. All we were doing was moving from the dreamscape to Faery.

Instead, we plummeted endlessly. I tried visualizing the bedroom. Tried a full-on travel spell. Nothing made a dent.

"Fix this," Zeke whined.

"Wish I could."

It was counterintuitive but perhaps it was only Faery that was closed to me. I held a picture of my last Coven in my mind's eye, the grounds and gardens. Once I had it, I switched destinations.

We tumbled out behind a brick wall in the Coven's herb garden. Two witches gasped in surprise. Before they could sound the alarm and circle the wagons, I scrambled over the wall and took off at a dead run, Zeke by my side and Sita flying.

I should still be asleep. How was any of this possible?

Had the witches locked onto my astral self? Or had they actually seen us all?

Beyond them, no one blinked as we pelted past. I hadn't cloaked us, so why weren't people squealing and pointing at Zeke? It added credence to the astral projection theory.

Panting, disoriented, dizzy, I led us between two old buildings. The alley stank of urine. I didn't care. Finding a dry spot, I sank to my haunches and wound invisibility around us.

"We have to go back," Sita cawed.

"We're not really here." Zeke sounded rattled.

"What do you mean?"

"You're asleep. This is a dream, but there's no straightforward way out." He howled. Two drunks bolted from the alley. They couldn't see us, but they'd certainly heard Zeke.

"There has to be. I'll try harder."

A quarter hour later, I'd cycled through every casting at my disposal, and we were still in the alley.

My head pounded. My mouth was dry. My stomach hurt so much I was afraid I might puke.

Was this how the sisterhood would finally win? By attrition? If I kept tossing spells into the ether, I'd run my reservoir dry.

"You can't stop," Zeke protested.

"I have to. For a while. What I'm doing isn't working. I need to sort through this."

He snuggled next to me. Sita stopped fussing and did the same. I put an arm around my wolf, shut my eyes, and slowed my breathing. Panic doesn't lend itself to clear thought.

For a time, I drifted. It was so much better than struggling, I gave into it. I was supposed to be asleep anyway. May as well go with the flow.

CHAPTER EIGHTEEN, DAMIEN

I caught up with everyone in our council chamber. Logan had convened an emergency meeting. Everyone's usual pleasant expressions were grim. Question was why. He glanced my way through narrowed silver eyes. "Good. I was just going to send someone to fetch you."

Questions brimmed over; I kept them all within the safety of my throat. I'd come in search of information, but it was prudent to listen. I didn't even have a seat on the council, much less a voice.

"Where is Morgan?" Maeve asked.

"Resting. We had a tough transit."

"While you were transiting, we had a visitor," Logan informed me.

I started to ask who, but didn't. He'd tell me soon enough.

"Not an actual in-the-flesh visitor," Maeve clarified.

That winnowed it down to someone magical, but who else would darken Faery's gates?

"Hermes showed up," Logan said flatly.

I hadn't bothered to find a seat. Good thing because shock battered me and I fell back a step.

"You went after Hecate," Logan went on.

I nodded. "You knew as much."

"What we didn't know," Maeve cut in, "was about your run in with Hermes."

I thought I'd told them, but realized I'd told Morgan and called it even. "Apologies. I should have mentioned it."

"You think?" Logan's tone was acidic.

Enough of this. He could bash me all he wanted, but, for now, we had more important details to cover. "What did he want?" I asked.

"He claims he told you to butt out of the witch problem."

Amidst a low chorus of *not our issue* from most of the council, I nodded agreement. "He did." I rolled my shoulders back. "Not half an hour ago, you offered up Faery's resources should Morgan and I have need of them. What happened?"

"We thought we'd only be facing witches," a woman on the council explained.

"We do not want dozens of angry Greeks bearing down on Faery," Logan said stiffly. "They could destroy our home, our lands."

I inhaled deeply, blew out a breath, and did it again to center myself. Calling my kinsmen a bunch of cowards would get me nowhere. Neither would pointing out there were scarcely dozens of Greeks. Perhaps a dozen or so who'd been consistently active. The rest were shadowy figures who'd left Earth eons ago.

"Did he say anything else?"

"Aye. If we persist meddling in witch business, we'll end up in a war." Logan sounded miffed, but it never has taken much to set him off.

"With whom?" I scribed circles in the air with my index finger.

"He didn't exactly say, but I presume he meant with the witches and a few annoyed Greek gods."

It seemed manageable, but I didn't point that out.

Maeve poked me. "Out with it. You're bursting to say something."

Good to have an opening, but how best to fill it?

"Hecate's been in Morgan's mind," I told them. Several pairs of eyes morphed from annoyance to surprise.

"On a whim," I continued, "I told her to latch onto the psychic energy and follow it. We nearly didn't make it out of there."

"Out. Of. Where?" Logan inserted spaces between his words. Usually equitable, he was as spun out as I'd ever seen him.

"I'm not completely certain. We ended up in one of the nasty psychic spaces between worlds. Hecate—if it really was her—lured Morgan with sweet words and music only she could hear. When Morgan didn't snap up the bait, the music turned harsh, and Hecate became strident and angry. Morgan said she seemed deranged."

"How'd you escape?" Maeve set her lips in a tight line.

"Not easily. It took both of us. Morgan wasn't sure she wanted to leave—"

"That's not good," Maeve snapped. "Means she was ensorcelled."

"How'd you get through to her?" Logan asked.

"I reminded her about Zeke and Sita back in Faery and pointed out if we didn't make a run for it, she'd never see them again."

"Did you feel a spell closing around you?" Maeve punctuated her question with a disgusted grunt.

"Something like that. Breaking through took everything both of us had."

"Never underestimate witches," Logan said. "We tend to think of them as substandard mages, but when you add in their dirty, stinking hex bags and their ticky-tacky spells, they control more skill than we give them credit for."

"After a rocky trip back, you left Morgan and the familiars alone?" A man on the council asked, the tips of his ears quivering with outrage at my carelessness.

"She's napping," I snapped.

"Are you sure about that?" Logan arched fair brows.

"If she was uncertain about leaving Hecate, perhaps she shooed you away to provide another opportunity to bond with her creator," the council member explained.

"You two should have activated the mate bond." Maeve spoke firmly. "It would have enhanced your joint abilities and allowed you to know where she is at all times."

I hadn't been the stumbling block throwing shade on

that plan. "I'm scarcely her jailer, but I'll go check on her. Did Hermes say anything else?"

"Wasn't the threat of war if we don't back down enough?" Logan sounded weary. We've been at peace since the 1500s. The specter of a full-on confrontation wasn't welcome.

"Witches aren't worth our time," someone called out. A susurrus of agreement rippled through the chamber.

"We've never made a habit of disparaging other mages," I reminded everyone and turned to leave before things became truly ugly.

"You have to tell her to stand down," Logan called after me.

Pivoting before I crossed beneath the lintel, I faced him. "I can tell her, but she won't listen. Morgan won't rest until she finds an endpoint."

"What will you do?" Maeve asked.

"I will support the woman I love."

"Even if it drags the rest of us into a war?"

How to answer her? "I will do everything I can to keep the Fae out of whatever unfolds, but I will not abandon Morgan."

"You may have to leave Faery," Logan said.

Whoa. Quantum leap from Faery's resources standing behind me to exile. I shook my head and stared at him. Probably should have kept my mouth shut, but restraint has never been my long suit.

"I cannot believe a simple visit from a Greek god had this effect on you. Since when are we a bunch of cravens hiding behind the illusion of an alliance? The Greeks were never our partners. Never. If we had an alliance with any of the gods, it was the Celts.

"Speaking of which, have we tried to raise any of them? Hermes might not be so quick to sling threats around if we had Danu in our court, or Arianrhod or Gwydion."

"Go check on your witch." Logan made shooing motions.

I got it. I'd raised an uncomfortable point, and now he wanted me gone.

Maeve's expression was unreadable, but then it often was.

I set a course for my rooms. Had Morgan given me the slip? Unlikely since she'd have been faced with what to do with Zeke and Sita. They'd given us a raft of shit for leaving them once. Neither would sit by idly and allow her to jump down a journey well.

The spicy scent of witch met me as soon as I walked through my door. Relief began at the tips of my ears and spilled through me. Taking care not to disturb her, I made my way to the bedroom.

Morgan sprawled on her side, mouth open breathing shallowly. Zeke lay next to her; Sita nestled in the curve of a collarbone. My impression about everything being all right imploded.

Zeke's eyes were open, but he wasn't moving. Ditto for the hawk. Normally, both animals would have greeted me.

My heart thudded against my ribcage; my throat was dry.

They were here, but not.

Why had Faery not kept them safe? Touching Morgan, I reached for her mind but ran into a black wall. Next, I rested a hand on Zeke's furry head. Images cascaded through my mind.

A dank alleyway.

The three of them huddled in the lee of a dumpster; Morgan's arms were crossed atop her knees. Her head rested on them, eyes shut.

The wolf looked up. *"Help us."*

"Where are you?"

"Trapped in a dream."

Sita noticed me and squawked weakly.

"What happened?"

"Morgan went to sleep. Hecate showed up. We tried to come back to Faery and ended up here."

At least Morgan hadn't run from me. Her only crime was falling asleep.

One of my magics is linked with the dreamworld. Would it be enough to find them?

"Are you close to anything familiar?" I asked the wolf.

"Coven guild house."

"Be there as soon as I can. If Morgan wakes, tell her to stay put."

A weak woof rustled through our link before it flickered out.

When I turned around, intent on gathering accoutrements for my journey, Maeve and Logan stood in the bedroom doorway.

"If you've come to tell me not to go after them, stuff it," I growled.

"I came to apologize," Logan said. "Your observation about the Greeks shamed me."

"And I came to see if anything was amiss." Maeve walked to Morgan and passed a hand over her forehead. Her frown deepened.

"What?" Concern, already running at Mach 10, flared hotter still.

"We have to find her, and damned soon."

I didn't ask why. Better not to know.

I tugged on a coat and rustled in a cabinet for healing powders, herbs to counteract the pull of the dreamworld.

"I'm coming," Maeve announced.

My head snapped in her direction. "If you want to help, fine. If you're offering to keep an eye on me, I don't require a nanny."

A spell built around her.

"You can't use a journey casting. Not for the dreamworld."

"What then?"

"I'll leave you to it," Logan interrupted. "Got to get back to the council. We liked your idea about raising one of the Celts, and we're working that angle."

"Have Bess and Zoe help you." Maeve named her two sister seers and released her nascent casting.

"Are you certain you want to come? It will be a rough ride," I said.

"Yes. You might need my ability."

She hadn't answered my question about her intentions,

but I've known Maeve a long time. She liked Morgan, and she's never meant me ill. I tugged out a futon tucked into the corner of my bedroom until it formed a double bed. Lying on it, I patted the spot beside me.

"We're going to enter the dreamscape," I explained. "The spell du jour will spin us to sleep. Once we're there, we can find Morgan and the animals."

"Do you have any idea where to look?"

"They're not far from the Coven guild house in Seattle. Narrows it down."

Maeve settled beside me. "I don't understand the nexus of the physical and dream worlds. Why would she be anywhere recognizable?"

"My guess is Morgan tried to get back into Faery. When she couldn't, she picked a destination that might allow her entry. It did, but she wasn't strong enough to escape the dreamer's paths."

As I spoke, worry deepened forming a crater in my mind. Not good. I needed all my faculties to pull this off.

Reaching for my connection to the Dream Guardian, an elusive Druid who's held the post for as long as my memory extends, I humbled myself and requested entry.

"Why not simply fall asleep?" a deep voice rumbled. His tall, bony frame swathed in blue robes formed in my mind's eye. Black hair was gathered in a thick queue at the nape of his neck. Dark eyes were set into deep sockets. A full beard covered his chest.

"One of my own is trapped. I must rescue her. Please allow me entrance to the dreamscape."

"Who is with you?"

"I am Maeve, seer to the Fae."

"Damien and Maeve"—his tone was formal—"you have one hour. It begins now. If you disturb the peace of this place, consequences will ensue."

My vision faded, leaving us in a dimly lit passageway.

"Come on." I ran until I located a stairway and started up it. Perhaps 500 steps later, we walked through a door and into muted daylight.

"Now we can use our normal magic," I told her and engaged a journey spell to spit us out near the Coven guild house.

"We're not in the usual world," she observed.

"Correct. This is the only way to transit through the dreamscape absent walking."

We came out on a familiar corner. I'd waited here for Morgan before. I caught a whiff of Zeke. Following him would buy us more than hunting for witch spoor. With the guild house so close, it would be easy to pick the wrong witch.

"It's like we're here, but not," Maeve muttered. "I had no idea any of this existed."

"Kind of like I had no idea you kept a secondary library. This way."

We didn't have to cover much distance before the alleyway came into view. So far, this had been easy, too easy.

Maeve laid a hand on my arm. "Careful," she breathed.

Either my apprehension was catching, or she'd felt something too. I tested the junction where the street ended and the alley began. It felt wrong somehow.

"Zeke. If you can, come to me."

Seconds later, his shaggy head popped out of the murk. Sita rode on his shoulders.

Maeve crouched and opened her arms. He ran into them. "Why didn't Morgan come with you?"

"Can't rouse her," Zeke whined.

"Worried," Sita cawed.

"This isn't good. I'm going in there," the seer mumbled as she straightened.

I thrust an arm in front of her. "No. Stay with the animals. I'll get Morgan."

"They don't care about me," Maeve insisted. "This is dangerous for you. The witches—and Kelpies and whoever else—want you out of the way."

"You saw this?"

At her terse nod, I stopped but not for long. Off and running, I sprinted down the alley.

A flow of Fae power tapped me from behind, circling me. Hard to fault Maeve for caring.

Buildings leaned inward, blocking out the pallid light of a gray day. The dreamworld muted available light still further. I dialed in my night vision and fired a mage light. It flared blue-white, a comforting presence in the gloom.

Morgan was exactly like I'd seen her when I connected through Zeke. Leaned against a brick wall, her eyes closed. An abrupt wakening could harm her, drive her into madness, so I was gentle, cautious as I slid my arms around her and lifted her.

Cradling her inert form against me, I started out of the alley.

A barrier stopped me. It hadn't been there moments before.

I turned the other way, and ran into another one.

Twisting back, I examined the first obstacle. Extending many feet above my head, its psychic weave was impenetrable. Waves of energy wafted from above it, probably what had immobilized Morgan.

How long did I have before it got me too? It hadn't impacted Zeke or Sita, so its influence must be specifically tuned.

Maeve and the animals ran toward us, stopping shy of the blockade. Sparks bounced off it as Maeve tested its integrity and worked on drilling through it. Holes opened but closed right back over. None of them were large enough to accommodate me.

I sent power of my own arcing at the obstacle. Morgan stirred in my arms, moaning softly. I coated her mind with calming spells to keep her unconscious.

Zeke ran at the weave, snapping and grabbing with his jaws. An unhappy yelp suggested the grid packed quite a punch. I hadn't tried touching it.

An idea took root. Using an enemy's power against them can be effective. Could I talk with Maeve?

"Can you hear me?"

She'd been facing sideways. Her head snapped in my direction. Excellent. Meant she could. I didn't think telepathy would work, not with the constant flow of wicked energy.

I walked right up next to the barrier. If she could hear me, so could anyone else who might be nearby. I retreated to the Fae's old language. It fell out of use millennia ago, but at least it wasn't likely to be intercepted.

The seer faced me from a foot away and turned her hands palms up.

"I'm going to channel the energy flowing from above. Once I have control, I'll cut through the weave. When the hole is big enough, reach through and grab Morgan. Be careful not to waken her."

"What about you?"

"I'll jump through, and we'll be gone."

"I can't pinpoint the source of that flow. It could damage you beyond repair," she cautioned.

At least Morgan would be safe. "Do you have a better idea?"

She shook her head. I laid Morgan as near the barrier as I dared and readied myself. The effects of the flow were already wearing on me. No time to waste.

Raising my arms above my head, I fashioned a capture spell and aimed it right at the flow. Obligingly, the rush of whatever it was came straight to my outstretched fingertips.

The shock, when it connected, was excruciating. Pain lacerated every nerve, every cell. If I'd caught fire, the agony wouldn't have been worse. I forced myself to think, to breathe, as I ran the side of my hand down the weave of the barrier from as far up as I could reach.

Christ! It hurt. Nothing has ever hurt me this much. Fire. Hot knives. Unseen teeth ripping at me.

The weave fell away. Through eyes that were losing focus, I saw Maeve snatch Morgan. Zeke stood watch over her while Maeve ducked through the hole I'd made and dragged me through it.

Dark power still thrummed along every sinew. I was screaming now because I couldn't hold them in. Flesh began sloughing off my bones, falling onto the ground in chunks of pink goo.

"Danu forgive me," Maeve cried just before everything went black.

CHAPTER NINETEEN, MORGAN

I woke in Damien's room feeling as if a truck had run over me. Zeke sat by the bed. Sita's talons were tangled in my hair.

Groaning, I rubbed my aching temples and staggered from the bed to the bathroom where I ran cold water into my cupped hands and dipped my face into it.

I did it over and over until my fingertips turned white and my teeth were chattering. Reconstructing what happened was tough. I remembered the track above the river and Hecate. With Faery closed to me, I'd fled to the Coven guild house to escape, but everything after that hazed over.

Zeke padded next to me while I was drying my face and hands. "What happened? I don't feel anything like myself."

"Damien and Maeve rescued us."

I massaged my aching temples. I'd sell my soul for aspirin. Probably no such thing in Faery.

"I don't get why we needed to be rescued. All I did was go to sleep."

The wolf crowded my side. His way of showing solidarity. When I returned to the bedroom and its rumpled bed, Sita cawed a greeting, but it was muted.

I looked from one to the other. "What happened? You're acting like someone died."

"Not dead." Maeve said briskly from the doorway, "but not doing especially well, either."

My heart skipped a few beats; my empty stomach cramped into a painful knot. Around a dry as dust throat, I sought clarification. "Damien?"

He wasn't here with me. It didn't bode well.

"Do you want to sit?" Maeve pointed at a chair.

"No." I swayed on my feet, alarmingly close to pitching facedown on the carpet.

The seer crossed the room, grabbed my arm, and directed me into the living room where she pushed me into a chair. Next, she thrust a glass of mead my way. "Drink this. You won't do anyone any good if you pass out."

My hands were shaking so badly I could scarcely guide the mug to my mouth. The amber liquid burned my mouth and throat and set my stomach on fire, but the panicky out-of-control sensation receded.

Maeve sat across from me. I squirmed beneath her scrutiny. One of her Fae was wounded, maybe near death, because of me. "Do you want me to leave?" I mumbled.

"And break Damien's heart after he sacrificed everything for you?"

"I give up. What do you want? Just tell me. I don't have the energy for guessing games."

"Don't you want to know what happened?"

"Of course I do."

Zeke pressed his body against my legs. *"She's not well,"* he protested.

"Neither is Damien," Maeve retorted.

I slugged back more mead, hoping for a boost to my flagging energy. All it did was make my aching head buzz unpleasantly.

"Witches and Kelpies trapped you in the dream realm," Maeve began. "When we found you, you were unconscious. Damien made certain you remained so to preserve your sanity."

"The animals?" I asked.

"Didn't affect them."

"When Damien tried to carry you out of the alley, he ran into a magical barrier. I couldn't drill through it."

"Just tell me. Don't drag this out."

"All right. He drew the flow powering the blockade into his own magical center. It allowed him to chop through it. I retrieved first you and then him. The sorcerous magic was eating him up from inside. He was literally burning up from within. I had to stop the destruction, so I sent him into a coma one step removed from death.

"He's with our healers, and they're doing what they can to extricate his essence from the dark magic he joined with."

"Surely, they can..." The look on her face stopped me.

My eyes burned with the hot prick of tears. Slowly, they

dripped down my cheeks. I didn't bother brushing them away.

"You must hate me." My voice was low, almost unrecognizable.

"No, child. How can I hate what was foretold."

Foretold. I raised my streaming eyes to her ice-blue gaze. "Do you know the outcome?"

Maeve shook her head. "By foretold, I meant your relationship with Damien." Her gaze sharpened. Out of her chair, she placed a hand first on my shoulder and then on my stomach. Fae enchantment churned through me. Amazement softened the seer's austere features.

"You carry his child. Did you know?"

Awk. The tears turned into a flood. I curved a hand over my belly and sent a tiny thread of power auguring inward. The beat of a new life, a son, was strong.

Zeke laid his head in my lap. *"I will welcome and protect the pack puppy."*

"I will welcome and protect him as well." Sita nestled in my lap between Zeke's snout and my stomach.

I was still sniveling like an idiot. I brushed against my wet cheeks. "Can I go to Damien."

"Of course. It might turn the tide. Naught else has."

"We're coming," Zeke announced.

"Yes, Morgan needs us now more than ever," Sita squawked.

My eyes flowed again. My pack. My family, but it was incomplete. How would we go on without Damien? His son needed him. We all did.

The trip to the Fae infirmary was a familiar one. My last

stint here, Mother had died under horrible circumstances, flesh sloughing off her bones. Not sure what I expected, the sight of Damien's wasted form beneath a light sheet sliced my heart into ruins.

Two Fae in their blue healer robes hovered over him, chanting softly. Runes filled the air, connecting and breaking apart as they danced to a drummer only they heard.

"Any change?" Maeve asked softly.

"Not really," one of the healers murmured.

A memory of witches telling me I was cursed blossomed. Maybe I shouldn't be here. Would I bring Damien bad luck too?

The other healer eyed me much the way Maeve had. "Are you—?" she began.

I nodded. "Just found out myself."

The healers exchanged a pointed look. "Come here." One beckoned to me. "Lie next to him."

"Under or over the sheet?"

Lacking my compunctions, Zeke jumped onto the bed and stretched full length against Damien's right side. Sita perched on the foot of the bed and rubbed her beak across both feet.

The healer turned the sheet back. I stifled a gasp. Damien's robust body had been reduced to skin stretched over bones. Large black patches covered parts of his thighs and chest. Was this where the eldritch power had burned him?

I started to lie down, but the healer said, "Take your clothes off. Skin to skin may save him."

I started to protest, to say I was too dirty to lie on their linens, but no one was sending me to the showers. Bending, I unlaced my boots. They still stank of urine from the alley. Next I removed my socks and unfastened my trousers. They pooled around my legs. A quick tug, and my jacket joined my other garments on the floor. My top slid over my head leaving only my underwear.

At a nod from the healer, I removed them too and lay next to Damien, curving my body around his. He was cold, so cold I wondered if they were wrong about him still being alive, but then I felt the rise and fall of his chest and laid my ear over his heart to hear its faint beat.

Sita relocated to his shoulders. Someone tossed a blanket over us.

"Maeve?" My voice was barely there, but she heard me.

"Aye, child."

"This spell you cast, the one that put him in a coma. Do you have to undo it?"

"I can't undo it. Either he will find his way back, or…"

Had there been any other choice? I didn't ask. She'd never have done something so radical if any other path had presented itself.

I tossed a leg over him and kept an arm around his chest. Nestling into the hollow of a collarbone, I breathed heat and life into the man I loved. I had no idea if he could hear me, but I reached for his magical center and twined my own with it.

"Damien. You have to try, darling. I love you. I cannot lose you. Reach for me. Reach for the light. We made a child. A son. He needs you. I need you. The animals are devastated. We're all

here with you. None of us want to go on without you. You saved my life. Let me save yours."

I repeated variations of my words over and over. With our magical centers tethered together, I explored the broken places in his body. I've never been a healer, but then I've never been a lot of other things, either.

Slowly, I sorted out parts that didn't belong. The healers intuited what I was about, and they removed the offending bits as I extricated them.

Hours passed. From time to time, someone brought me water or a piece of fruit, but then I returned to my task. Finally, I couldn't find any more poison. His heartbeat was stronger, but he was still sunk deep in the Fae death coma.

I dozed off and on, but I refused to give up.

At one point, when I returned from a trip to the bathroom, I asked the healer, a different one so they must rotate much like nurses do, "How long have I been here?"

She smiled softly. "A few days. Perhaps a week. He is getting stronger."

I settled back next to Damien. The sheets smelled of lavender. Someone had changed them. Zeke and I traded sides periodically. Sita barely left long enough to peck at the dish of seeds someone had put out for her.

I don't think Zeke ate anything.

Beyond the healers, Maeve, Logan, or one of the council was always here. Maybe they didn't trust me, or maybe they were worried about Damien. So far, the curse—if there really was one—hadn't reared its ugly head.

More time passed. I had no idea how much.

My eyes were closed as I communed with the babe

within me. Even at his young age, he had fully formed thoughts. What would his magic look like? Would he favor the Fae? Probably, since there weren't any male witches. There would have been except we killed them off in infancy. Who knew what their magic would have matured into.

For the first time, I asked myself why male witches were nipped in the bud. Was there some ugly secret I didn't know about. I'd ask Maeve, but not now.

I was half asleep, exhorting Damien to come back to us when I heard, "Morgan." Half rasp, half whisper, it sent me upright hunting for its source.

The healers on duty mobbed the bed. "He's awake," one cried.

I studied the man I'd held in my arms for weeks. His eyes fluttered open. A weak smile illuminated his wasted features.

Sobs rocked me to my core. When he opened his arms, I dove into them. I had no words. We just held one another. Zeke licked him up one side and down the other. Sita snuggled close, cooing like a dove.

We were a family again.

For the first time in a while, my thoughts turned to something beyond calling Damien back from the gates of the dead. Or maybe the gates of the *Dreaming* since it's where the Fae go when they tire of living.

What had transpired while we were shut off from the world in the infirmary? Had Hecate stormed the gates? Were the Fae at war with witches or, worse, the Greek gods? No one had given me any news, not that I'd asked for it.

Damien had been my sole focus.

It was selfish of me, but, with him back, nothing else mattered. My single-minded pursuit of Hecate was over. I was done with an endeavor that had nearly been the death of my love.

And me.

Reality jabbed hard. I only hoped I was done. Maeve had suggested everything was foretold. Walking away to skirt elements that had been put in play the moment I was made might not be as easy as I envisioned.

For now, I'll nurse Damien back to health and pretend everything is normal.

We'll see how far it gets me.

CHAPTER TWENTY, DAMIEN

Once I shook off the dregs of Maeve's spell, I recovered quickly. In a few weeks, the lesions marking my body receded. I gained weight. The fuzziness plaguing my mind went away, and I felt like the old version of me.

Best of all, Morgan was by my side every step of the way. We took long walks in Faery and talked about everything from magic to history. We spent time in my beloved library. Once the healers pronounced I was fit enough to leave the infirmary, she and I whiled away hours exploring one another's bodies.

Beyond lust, tenderness and compassion grew between us.

I was in love with our child to be. With my hand on Morgan's belly, I talked with him, got to know him. It would be months yet before his birth, but I couldn't wait to be a father.

Had his life force been waiting in the wings? I hadn't asked Maeve if she'd seen our son in her crystals, but for him to appear after our very first lovemaking must mean something.

I wanted to join Logan and the other Fae at council meetings, but he wouldn't allow it until I was fully healed. Claimed he didn't want to impede my progress. No one spelled it out, but they'd all been plenty worried about me.

I must have been in dire straits for Maeve to resort to placing me in a coma. But I'd saved Morgan. It was what I'd set out to do, and my gambit had worked, albeit with a rather high price tag.

Morgan and the animals and I fell into a comfortable pattern. During Faery's nights, Zeke and Sita hunted just beyond the veils separating us from Earth. It afforded privacy for cuddles, snuggles, and passion hot enough to scorch my soul. Unlike Morgan, I'd been far from virginal, but the heated longing igniting every cell was brand new.

Sex had been a release before. I'd cared about my partners, but we'd been clear our dalliances would remain on the physical plane and either of us could walk away any time.

Sex with Morgan was different. It bound us, one to the other. If I asked her again about the mating ceremony, I was certain she'd say yes this time.

She rolled over, tucking her body around mine in her sleep. The easy rise and fall of her breathing tickled my neck. Was she dreaming? No harm to peek. We shared everything, after all.

Ever so gently, I snuck beneath the curtain of her mind.

And froze.

Where I'd expected rainbows and unicorns and pastel colors, what I found was a grim-faced witch bent over a large text and a kettle. The book smelled of sheep, and the vellum had worn away from much usage. Morgan sat on the far side of the table, and the two women were deep in conversation.

Greasy black hair, thinner than Morgan's, formed a shroud that ended on the floor.

How was I so certain the woman was a witch?

What else could she be? They're the ones who use grimoires and kettles.

My body must have stiffened, turned less welcoming.

"Hey, sleepyhead." Morgan tousled my long hair from her spot wrapped around behind me.

"Hey, yourself." I worked at sounding normal.

"What's wrong?"

How could I tell her I'd snooped on her dreams and found someone who looked a hell of a lot like Hecate. I hadn't seen her eyes. They're a dead giveaway with their copper irises and deep green centers.

"Nothing. Trying not to disturb you."

"You could never disturb me." She tugged on my shoulder to roll me over.

Lovemaking would come next, except I've never felt less like intimacy. Morgan had to know about the fell presence in her dreams.

Why hadn't she mentioned it?

I'd stupidly assumed we had no secrets, yet this was a

huge omission. Even if it wasn't Hecate, having any witch in her dreams didn't bode well. For her or for us.

Protectiveness for our unborn son surged. Witches would kill him.

Morgan tugged harder. "Are you all right? You're not having a relapse, are you? The healers warned me about—"

I rolled over and smiled, aiming for reassuring. "I'm fine."

Fingertips strayed down my chest and belly, arrowing for my cock. Why wouldn't they? We made love every morning until Zeke and Sita returned.

Still creeped out from my snooping and uncertain why I didn't come out and ask her what was going on, I laid a hand over hers stopping its downward trajectory.

"Maybe I am a wee bit under the weather this morning. Naught to be concerned about."

Twin lines formed between her eyebrows. "Why'd you lapse into Gaelic."

Oops. "Wasn't aware I had. Your command of it has mostly returned."

She closed her teeth over her lower lip. "Not exactly my point. Um, do you want breakfast?"

Why was I so loathe to just out and ask her?

Because no answer she could provide would be satisfactory. Nothing she could say would protect our son from falling into witchy clutches.

We'd accepted Morgan into our midst. Was she hiding behind the guise of love and partnership to plot mayhem? At the end of the day, she was still Hecate's get. Surely, that loyalty...

I rolled away from Morgan and got out of bed. The chamber smelled faintly of last night's lovemaking. Usually, it aroused me, but not today.

"Damien?"

I felt the probe of her enchantment as she attempted to look into my mind. On her feet, she faced me. The gentle curve of belly and breasts reminded me of the babe growing within.

I grabbed a robe off a hook, shrugged into it, and tossed another her way. "We need to talk."

"What about?"

Did I detect a worried note beneath her question? Or was I imagining things?

Stalling for time, I heated a kettle with a shot of magic and poured steaming water over mixed tea leaves. The blend *du jour* was rosemary and mint. She'd fallen silent and withdrawn her exploratory mission to cull my thoughts.

Before I could motion her to a chair, she said, "You found out." Her tone was flat, unreadable.

"Maybe. What exactly do you think I discovered?"

Morgan tilted her head at a defiant angle. "Hecate. She visits my dreams sometimes."

"And you failed to mention this, why?" Those words cost me. What I wanted to do was yell, shriek, and pound holes in the walls.

"Because it would have upset you."

"How long?"

"Since we moved back into your rooms." Morgan's mismatched gaze fell before whatever she saw oozing from me.

My hands had curled into fists. I stretched out my fingers long enough to slug back some tea.

"Has she been riding shotgun while we made love?"

"No. Of course not. I'd never have allowed it."

"How would you have known? Dream world channels are difficult to close once opened." Words refused to stop despite me doing my damnedest to hang onto them. "This whole mess began when you were trapped in the dreamscape. By Hecate. At the first breath of her in your dreams, you should have sounded an alarm."

"She claims it wasn't her but the witches and Kelpies holding me prisoner."

"And you believed her?" Incredulity underscored my words.

"Had no reason not to," she mumbled, eyes still downcast.

I set my mug on a table before I cracked it.

"I can't even talk with you about this," I sputtered. "You hid it for a reason."

Morgan rolled her shoulders back and glared at me through narrowed eyes. "Yes. *This* was the reason. I knew precisely how you'd react. She told me to keep this between us, and—"

"You worked this out with Hecate?" I thundered. "Why not with me. I'm supposed to be your mate, your love."

"Not mates."

"Aye, and a damned good call. Being tethered to a lying conniving—"

Stop right there, my inner voice jumped into the fray. I turned away from Morgan, breathing hard.

Zeke and Sita chose that moment to return. After one look at us, they turned tail and went back through the door.

"She's not what you think," Morgan insisted.

"She's ensorcelled you," I hissed.

"Talk with her. Join us in my dreams."

"Ha. So I can end up back in the Fae death coma? No thank you."

Tears sheened Morgan's eyes. "I can't give either one of you up. It's why I didn't tell you."

"Because you knew damned good and well what my reaction would be."

She nodded.

Loathe to touch her, I moved near enough to place a hand over her stomach. The words of an ancient spell fell from my lips. I was nearly done before horror turned Morgan's features into a mask.

"Nooooo," she shrieked. "You cannot."

"I just did. Enough of the casting is done. It ensures I hold sovereignty over the child. He is mine, and he will be raised as one of the Fae. What were you thinking, Morgan? Witches kill male children."

"Not on my watch, they wouldn't. Good luck finding us." Morgan shucked the robe and began tossing clothes on.

"Blood calls to its own. I will find him once he is born. The spell I just wove guarantees your cooperation." I paused long enough for rationality to intrude. "The only reason you recognized that particular casting is because Hecate must have intervened. She's not only in your dreams, but she also lives within you during your waking moments."

Morgan refused to look at me. It was all the answer I needed.

My heart ached. My soul had been cast asunder. I'd mourn later. Now was the time to ensure the snake in the grass I'd tethered myself to couldn't harm my people. Or my son.

Dressed, she tossed her few possessions into a leather valise.

I started to ask where she'd go, how she'd survive, but it wasn't my place to know.

She slung her bag over one shoulder.

"What will you tell the animals?"

Breath shuddered from her. "The truth."

"Then also tell them they are welcome with me."

"Would you rob me of everything?"

The anguish in her words smote me. I held firm. "It's not me robbing you of anything, but your own actions. I want to ensure they are safe if they can't stomach your complicity any longer."

She flinched.

I wanted to take my words back, except I'd spoken true.

"Is there any way—?" she began in a small voice.

"I don't trust you." So much more I wanted to say. I sat on all of it. No reason to prolong this.

She choked back a sob, waved a hand, and vanished.

My tears were far too near the surface for comfort. I sank into a crouch; the tatters of my hopes and dreams taunted me.

How could she have invited Hecate into our midst?

How could she have jeapordized our son?

How could I not have known?

Because it was simpler not to look. Perhaps, in my heart of hearts, I'd known all along.

None of it mattered. I'd move forward. In a few months, I'd collect my son. Claiming him had been harsh, reactive, yet, had I not done so, I'd never have seen him.

And the witches would have killed him.

Being cloaked in doing the right thing was cold comfort. Still, it was all that was left to me.

I was still crouched with my arms wrapped around my knees when Sita flew into the room and landed on my shoulder.

"Zeke would have come," she cawed, "but he cannot leave Morgan no matter what. It's how the familiar bond works."

I stroked her feathers, grateful for her loyalty. I'd saved her life once; she hadn't forgotten.

We were still huddled like that when Maeve pushed into my chamber. "Get up. The council requires your presence."

I stood, still cradling the hawk in my arms. "You know?"

"More than you imagine. Now get moving."

I handed Sita to her while I shucked my robe and donned trousers, a tunic, and soft leather shoes. Whatever the council had in mind, I was still Fae. They might blame me for entering into a relationship outside the bonds of our people. But in the end, I'd done the right thing.

I'd accept whatever blame they heaped on my head. Accept it and move forward.

Maeve turned and walked out of my rooms, still holding Sita. I followed. The sooner I got past whatever lay ahead, the sooner I could begin the long, slow process of reconstructing my life, my dignity.

I'd miss Morgan forever, but this wasn't about me. She'd made her choices. Now I was making mine. The world is a harsh mistress, but I'd get past the pain cleaving me in two. Someday, I'd be whole again.

Soon, I'd find my boy and bring him home.

You've reached the end of *Cursed*, second of the Bound by Shadows books. If you enjoyed it, please take a moment to leave a review. They mean so much to authors and are an opportunity for you to let other readers know what you loved about this book.

Look for *Promised* soon. An excerpt from it follows.

BOOK DESCRIPTION, PROMISED:

Magic runs strong in me, but power isn't enough.

Actually, these days nothing is enough. I've done a fine job alienating everyone who ever cared about me from the witches in my Coven, to the man I love, to my wolfie familiar. Mother's familiar left, winging a path to Faery. My wolf made it abundantly clear he'd have gone with her except the familiar bond doesn't allow that level of latitude.

He howled up a storm about being stuck with me, and quit talking.

Meanwhile, the babe growing within me is equally silent. He misses Damien's soothing voice, mandolin, and Fae love. I'm under a geas to return my son to Faery the second he's born. Ha! They'll have to find me first. No power words in the universe will make me relinquish my boy.

Hecate still rattles around in my mind. I'm done with her. If I hadn't allowed her in, I'd still be in Faery with Damien's arms around me.

Woulda. Coulda. Shoulda. Talk is cheap.

Pregnant. Nowhere to call home. No money. Nothing but my magic. Somehow, it will have to carry us through.

PROMISED, CHAPTER ONE, MORGAN

I left Faery in a huff because I was too humiliated to endure the look on Damien's face a moment longer. Betrayal twisted his features into harsh planes that shattered my world. My temper has never been my friend, and I was devastated—and mortified—he'd uncovered my secret.

To avoid lashing out and accusing him of snooping where he had no business, I took off. Not that I had any moral high ground, none at all. I was at fault. No apology in the world would make up for this particular fall from grace.

Keeping Hecate's visits to my psyche under wraps was unrealistic; thinking I could was stupid. It wasn't that I never planned to reveal her presence, but I needed more time. Damien had nearly died because of a plot spawned by witches and the Greek gods.

Except he's convinced Hecate was behind it.

I don't know anymore. About much of anything. She swore she was innocent, but she's scarcely an uninterested party in this game. She's locked behind iron shielding on a border world.

I'm her only hope of escape. At least, that's her story.

"You sure fucked that up," Zeke snarled, not bothering with mind speech. His words were garbled, but after all the centuries we've spent together, I don't have trouble understanding him. He's a huge white wolf and my bonded familiar.

"How could you?" Sita squawked and came as close as she ever has to jamming her beak into me. A large hawk with russet plumage, she'd been Mother's familiar.

We weren't far from the veils separating Earth from Faery, mostly because I had no idea where to go. Part of me hoped Damien would come after me, but a bigger part knew he never would. I'd wounded him beyond forgiveness. All he wanted was to rip our child from my womb and get on with his life.

Could I make my familiars understand my side of the equation? Both of them were glaring at me. It was worth a shot, but animals place loyalty above all else. From their perspective, mine should have favored Damien. Instead, I'd snuck behind his back to visit Hecate.

"I felt torn," I began. "She made me."

"So?" Sita clacked her beak. "Not as if you didn't have a perfectly good mother."

Ouch. I winced. Mother was dead. Because of me. So far, Sita had avoided casting blame. I girded myself for a barrage of accusations.

Tears threatened to spill over. I truly was cursed. The witch who'd thrown it in my face spoke true.

"You should have told Damien." Zeke's howl was full of reproach.

"I was hunting for the right time—"

"The only time was right after she showed up," Sita cawed. "I'm done. Your mother would be appalled by your behavior."

"Done? What do you mean?" My voice shook.

"I'm going back to Damien." Screeching like a mad thing, she wheeled and flew toward the veils.

"I'd go too, if I could." Zeke turned his back on me, hackles fully displayed.

"I won't hold you," I said stiffly. If I was going to lose everything, may as well get it over with.

"Unlike you"—he was still snarling—*"I value honor above my own desires."*

Aw crap. Could he have aimed his blow any harder? I already felt like the lowest of the low.

"What's the point if we can't work together?" My words were ragged because my throat housed an enormous lump.

"I will do what I must, but nothing more. Stop talking. You disgust me."

I sank into a crouch, hands folded over my belly, but the usually chatty babe was silent as well. They all hated me, but I deserved it.

"You handled that splendidly, my dear." Hecate was back, sounding positively jovial. So delighted, perhaps she'd dropped the idea in Damien's head to spy on my dreams.

"Go away," I moaned.

"You don't mean that. We're finally rid of that pesky Fae. Now we can get down to the real work."

"Which is?" I inquired acidly.

"I can't believe you even asked that," Zeke growled.

Come to think of it, neither could I.

"I'm confused," I told the witch goddess. "Until I see a clear path forward, I'm not doing anything for you."

"Confused about what?" Compulsion, warm as heated mead, swirled through my mind.

"Everything. Who you are. Whose side you're on. Whether you were responsible for Damien's accident." I was on a roll, so I kept on going. "I don't know you—at all. You plotted with Mother to create me, and then you were gone."

"You know I was held against me will." More compulsion, slithery and inviting.

I wound a ward around my mind.

"I don't know anything. Surely, there was a window between my making and your imprisonment. Yet, you did nothing. Leave me alone. I know where you are if I change my mind."

"I'm the only one who can mitigate the geas, so we can keep your son."

"We?" I yelped. "What in the fuck do you have to do with him?"

"Why I'd planned on raising him with you. Male witches have untapped power. Nearly as potent as your own. Speaking of which—"

I snugged up the weave of my ward and blocked her. It would hold for a while, but not forever.

"No need to put on an act on my account." Zeke still faced away from me.

"I'm not putting on an act," I protested. "She's how I got into this mess, and—"

"No. You're how you got into it," Zeke spoke over me.

Out of the mouths of wolves.

"We can debate this later. I'm going to find a place to hole up for a few days."

"Did you take the Fae money?"

He was referring to a sack containing money, ID, and credit cards the Fae had given me before one of my sojourns. I shook my head. "Of course not. What do you take me for?"

He shrugged his furry shoulders. *"Not sure who you are. Still figuring it out."*

His words cut deep. Trust is a funny thing. Until it's gone, you assume it has resilience when it's actually as fragile as butterfly wings.

Zeke fell silent. I played options through my mind. The boardinghouse where I'd met Damien was out. I'd killed five witches there, and the local Paranormal Detective Agency was keeping a close eye on the place. Maybe the cabin in the southern Cascades where we'd gone right after that could work. Damien had known about it, but it wasn't "his" place.

He'd never look for me there.

Hell, he wasn't ever going to seek me out again. The reality carved a hole in my heart. I'd loved him. Still did, and I probably always would. Wanting nothing more than to fall on my face and lick my wounds, I gathered the strands of a journey spell, calling them to me.

"Where are we going?" Zeke sounded suspicious.

"The cabin where we went after we left the boarding house. Do you have a better idea?" I've always included him in important decisions, and I wasn't about to stop now.

He didn't answer, so I edged nearer him and launched my casting.

Moments later, we emerged into midafternoon sunshine in front of the primitive hut where we'd stayed before. This would be hard. Damien's scent still lingered in the air. It would be thicker inside. Not ready to face never holding him again, I sat on the front steps, folded my arms across my knees, and laid my head over them.

Zeke ran off, presumably to hunt. Or because he couldn't stand being near me. No one else could. Why should he be any different?

A presence skulked at the edges of my ward. Hecate. Damn it. She'd never give up no matter how many ways I said no.

"May as well get used to it," I muttered and got to my feet. I could do a better job holding her at bay inside because I'd wrap enchantment around the building. It would add space around me, which should make it more difficult for her to penetrate my warding.

I scanned the wooded glen around the cottage. Birds dotted tree branches. Rabbits popped their heads up from time to time. I should do a spot of hunting, but food was the last thing on my mind. Anything I ate would probably come right back up the shape my gut was in.

Eventually, I'd have to do my best to choke something down for the child. I placed protective hands over my gently swelling belly. I was about three months along. Witch pregnancies are usually ten months with mortal fathers. Hard to say how long this one would last.

Reaching inward, I searched for my son's mind. It was closed to me. After weeks of open communication, his abrupt dismissal poured salt into my raw emotions.

He'd heard Damien's power words, knew he'd leave my side as soon as the Fae could track me down. Was he in favor of leaving my side?

Awk. Did any of it even matter?

I've been a lot of things in my thousand odd years, but dispirited isn't one of them. I've always picked myself up, dusted myself off, and played the ball where it laid. Even Mother's death didn't flatten me like Damien's dismissal and my familiar's harsh words.

"Stop. Just stop." I spoke aloud to steady myself and trudged up the cabin's few steps. The door was sealed with magic: Damien's magic. I stopped to inhale the pine forest scent of his workings.

Tears welled. I brushed them aside, broke the seal, and walked inside.

Nothing had changed. A small stack of my possessions, my notebook, and some of Damien's magical accoutrements were still here, protected by magic I'd layered over them. A scrap of paper I'd left for him that said, *Looking for you* had been tucked over the mantle.

Hecate was close. Too close.

My first order of business was blocking her out of my business. I took more care than I do with most of my castings, winding layer upon layer around the humble hut. When I was done, I couldn't sense her.

Misery gnawed a hole in my soul. I sank into the only chair. An image of sharing it with Damien while he held me close mocked me. Since I couldn't obliterate it, I let it float by.

I must have dozed because the angle of light filtering through the only window had sharpened, changed when I next looked at it. Zeke wasn't back. Who knew if he'd ever return.

Loyalty be damned. He could have easily changed his mind.

On my feet, I layered kindling into the fireplace and lit it with a thought. Once it was burning well, I added one of two larger pieces from the hearth. I'd have to go outside and gather more wood, or it would be a chilly night.

Outside.

If I were quick, perhaps Hecate wouldn't notice I'd emerged from my cocoon.

Fat fucking chance. She's nothing if not opportunistic as fuck. About the only truth in her longwinded diatribes, peppered with visions of retribution, had been she required my magic to extricate herself from the borderworld. She couldn't force my cooperation, but she could make my life a living shitshow when I kept on refusing.

Determined not to let her rule my life, I wrapped my mind in shielding and marched out of the cabin. For a few minutes, I thought I'd outfoxed her, but on my third trip gathering downed wood, the telltale scratching started again.

I hustled back up the steps thinking I really should call Zeke. He was a weak spot. Maybe. Unsure how long her current reach was, I went with "better safe than sorry," raised my mind voice, and called my familiar.

He didn't answer, but I hadn't expected him to.

Heart thudding against my ribcage, I tried again. This time, I added to my sending. *"Please. It's not safe."*

Even with him furious at me, he was still my responsibility. I didn't tell him that. It would have wounded his pride—and made him even less likely to come to me.

I dumped the armload of wood inside the door and stood on the porch scanning every nook and cranny in thick foliage as light leached out of the day. With each passing minute, panic threatened to swamp me.

I could not lose Zeke, no matter how he felt about me. I'd told him to leave, but I hadn't meant it. Not really. Hecate wasn't above using him as a pawn to get to me.

He and I should have talked about that.

Raising a fist, I shook it at the sky. "If you fuck with me," I gritted, "I will never help you do shit. Leave my familiar out of this."

"I made him too." Her voice was faint, but she'd broken through.

Goddamn it.

A flurry of white fur burst into the clearing. I ran to him. "Are you all right? She didn't hurt you, did she?"

He tossed a blood streaked snout. *"A bit late to care about unintended consequences, isn't it?"* After shaking himself from nose to tail tip, he stalked past me and up the stairs.

"Leave us the hell alone," I shouted and bounded into

the cabin, slamming the door and resurrecting the part of my spell encompassing it.

Zeke glared at me from a corner. He lay with his head on his paws and cleaned gore off his fur. Appeared the hunting had been a success.

At least one of us had a full belly. Except I still didn't feel the least bit like eating.

"Don't be selfish. The child needs food."

I busied myself stacking wood on the hearth and feeding the fire. "I'll eat tomorrow."

"How long will we be here?"

"I don't know. Not long. I'll work on a more permanent solution."

"Here is all right. Lots of game." Done cleaning himself, he curled into a ball and shut his eyes.

He'd weighed in.

There were worse places. And we were already here. I picked through the small bundle of possessions we'd left our first time here. Except the *we* part had changed.

After plucking a few crystals from Damien's stash, I tucked them close to my body, wrapped myself in a thick coat, and returned to the chair leaving the bed for Zeke if he wanted it.

Notebook and pen in hand, I settled in to write an honest account of Hecate's visitations. When she first showed up, what she'd said, what I replied. If the notebook ever fell into Damien's hands, he'd have the truth.

All of it.

To ensure believability, I laced a truth spell into the pages. It would glow, proving the veracity of my words.

Bending to my task, I began.

The first night after we moved back into your rooms after your illness, Hecate came to me. She expressed joy about your recovery and about our unborn son. She told me witches and the Greeks had finessed the barrier that was nearly the death of you.

I had no reason to disbelieve her...

About the Author

Ann Gimpel is a USA Today bestselling author. A lifelong aficionado of the unusual, she began writing speculative fiction a few years ago. Since then her short fiction has appeared in many webzines and anthologies. Her longer books run the gamut from urban fantasy to paranormal romance. Once upon a time, she nurtured clients. Now she nurtures dark, gritty fantasy stories that push hard against reality. When she's not writing, she's in the backcountry getting down and dirty with her camera. She's published over 100 books to date, with several more planned for 2023 and beyond. A husband, grown children, grandchildren, and wolf hybrids round out her family.

Keep up with her at https://www.anngimpel.com or https://www.anngimpelaudiobooks.com

If you enjoyed what you read, get in line for special offers and pre-release special reads. Newsletter Signup!

ALSO BY ANN GIMPEL

SERIES

Alphas in the Wild

Hello Darkness

Alpine Attraction

A Run for Her Money

Fire Moon

Bitter Harvest

Deceived

Twisted

Abandoned

Betrayed

Redeemed

Bound by Shadows

Scarred

Cursed

Promised

Cataclysm

Harsh Line

Warped Line

Cracked Line

Broken Line

Highland Secrets

To Love a Highland Dragon

Dragon Maid

Dragon's Dare

Dragon Fury

Earth Reclaimed

Earth's Requiem

Earth's Blood

Earth's Hope

Elemental Witch

Timespell

Time's Curse

Time's Hostage

Gatekeeper

Shadow Reaper

Rebel Reaper

Untamed Reaper

GenTech Rebellion

Winning Glory

Honor Bound

Claiming Charity

Loving Hope

Keeping Faith

Ice Dragon

Feral Ice

Cursed Ice

Primal Ice

Magick and Misfits

Court of Rogues

Midnight Court

Court of the Fallen

Court of Destiny

Rubicon International

Garen

Lars

Soul Dance

Tarnished Beginnings

Tarnished Legacy

Tarnished Prophecy

Tarnished Journey

Soul Storm

Dark Prophecy

Dark Pursuit

Dark Promise

Underground Heat

Roman's Gold

Wolf Born

Blood Bond

Wayward Mage

Hands of Fate

Jinxed

Hunted

Salvaged

Tiana

Wolf Clan Shifters

Alice's Alphas

Megan's Mates

Sophie's Shifters

Wylde Magick

Gemstone

Lion's Lair

Unbalanced

STANDALONE BOOKS

Branded, That Old Black Magic Romance (paranormal romance)

Edge of Night (short story collection, paranormal and horror)

Grit is a 4-Letter Word (nonfiction)

Heart's Flame (post-apocalyptic romance)

Icy Passage (science fiction romance)

Marked by Fortune (post-apocalyptic coming of age story)

Melis's Gambit (historical paranormal romance)

Midnight Magic (paranormal romance)

Red Dawn (post-apocalyptic paranormal romance)

Shadow Play (historical paranormal romance)

Shadows in Time (Highland time travel romance)

Since We Fell (contemporary romance)

Warin's War (paranormal romance)